Playing Hard to Forget

Piper Doone

Dreamspinner Press

Published by
DREAMSPINNER PRESS

5032 Capital Circle SW, Suite 2, PMB# 279, Tallahassee, FL 32305-7886 USA
http://www.dreamspinnerpress.com/

Playing Hard to Forget
© 2014 Piper Doone.

Cover Art
© 2014 L.C. Chase.
http://www.lcchase.com
Cover content is for illustrative purposes only and any person depicted on the cover is a model.

ISBN: 978-1-63216-887-0
Digital ISBN: 978-1-63216-294-6
Library of Congress Control Number: 2014953638
First Edition December 2014

Printed in the United States of America
∞
This paper meets the requirements of
ANSI/NISO Z39.48-1992 (Permanence of Paper).

To Amanda

PROLOGUE

A THOUSAND years ago, when the world was dark and ruled by myths and magic, a young man happened upon the Forest of Stocket in what would become Aberdeen, Scotland.

He was an ordinary man, a family man, a hunter, a fisher, a Robertson. The forest was home to creatures he could bring to his children and wife for food, for the warmth of their fur. He set about his journey with his *sgian-dubh*, his small knife just sharp enough to cut through the belly of a bird or cut a fruit from its tree.

This ordinary, relatively unarmed man, Struan, made his way deeper into the forest, chasing after rabbits. Suddenly he heard a terrible commotion in a small clearing. A flash of blue and a low, menacing growl alerted Struan to the presence of a wolf.

The wolf had a man cornered. He was certain to die if Struan did not intervene. The darkness of late dusk afforded Struan the element of surprise, and armed only with his *sgian-dubh*, he slayed the wolf, laying its corpse at the feet of the trapped man in victory.

Now, as all great folktales go, the man Struan saved that night was no random traveler through the woods. He was, in fact, King Malcolm II. Struan was rewarded with land, a title, and a castle—riches beyond compare for the eleventh century. He was heralded a hero, the bravest man in the land.

But, as great folktales also often go, that wasn't the end of the story for Struan and the wolf.

Morning came in the Forest of Stocket, and a family of forest dwellers by the name of Kinnaird came upon the horrific sight of a wolf's head upon a pike, right at the exact spot where Struan had killed him. They had smelled the blood for miles and chased down its scent until they found the source.

The woman immediately collapsed at the base of the pike, wailing an unnatural, inhuman howl. The children and elders joined in, for they knew this wolf.

Husband.

Father.

Son.

Werewolf.

And so began a war that has lasted a millennium. The small pack of wolves vowed to seek revenge on Struan Robertson and his family. Many died in the first battles. Those who survived—on both sides—bore children, grew their families, and trained them in the ways of killing and survival. Their numbers grew and spread throughout the world, not just Robertsons and Kinnairds, but humans and wolves who proved their loyalties and their skills. Each generation was born in battle and lived only to fight and discover better ways to kill.

It waged on through revolutions and wars and times of peace and enlightenment. It waged on through the discovery and settlement of the United States, with secret battles that would put Civil War skirmishes to shame.

Blind vengeance ruled the battlefields until treaties and truces were drafted. They rarely lasted a generation, but over the centuries, some basic laws came about that both sides agreed to. Numbers were dwindling on both sides, and neither wanted to be the first to die out.

Unprovoked attacks were subject to death without retaliation. Children were strictly off limits. Those who operated outside protective packs or families were not subject to the protection of the laws. Wolves and humans not involved were to be left alone, but if they got in the way, if they attacked, they were fair game to kill or turn.

It was an honor to be a Robertson. An honor passed down to each new generation, and an honor earned by each new generation. They married only the best, fiercest hunters from all walks of life to ensure their children's success, in hopes that it would be them who slayed the last Kinnaird.

It was an honor all Robertson heirs took seriously from the moment they were able to handle a weapon, and this unwavering loyalty has never faltered for a thousand years.

PART 1

CHAPTER 1

1991

FIONA ROBERTSON flopped in, as she always did, her blonde hair in a mess and her big blue eyes threatening to roll out of her fifteen-year-old head. Her big brother, Ethan, pretended he couldn't feel the entire bed shake as she announced her entrance, and instead tried to look really interested in his math work. She gave him a generous five seconds before she harrumphed loudly and rolled onto her back like an attention-starved puppy.

"What is it, Fi?" His tone matched his own steely blue eyes, but he could not resist his little sister for long.

"Uuunngh.... Dad. God. He made me shoot for *hours*, Ethan. Nothing but groupings and follow-through and ugh. I broke a nail." She looked positively put out as she shoved the offending digit in his face.

He batted it away because he just did not have time for the melodrama. "Fi, come on now. I've got better things to do than lament the loss of your perfect manicure. You knew Dad was taking you out to shoot this afternoon. I don't know why you bother. Archery and pretty pink nails just don't go together. Now leave me alone. Not all of us in this house are lucky enough to have summer off from school." As if Ethan had needed another reminder that his social life had slipped away before he really even had the chance to have one.

Fiona scooted herself to the edge of the bed like she was going to leave, but instead hung her head off and started framing the upside-down room with her fingers in front of her eye in a triangle shape.

"Yeah, not all of us are nerds who go to college 365 days a year. I don't know why you bother. It's not like Dad is going to let us be anything but hunters."

Ethan sighed because, yeah, she was annoying him, but also because she was right. But he had always been a "plan B" kind of guy and it turned out he had quite the aptitude for math.

"Fi." He kicked her feet upward with his so she tumbled in a graceless backward roll off the bed. "Go."

Fiona stood and adjusted herself, shooting him a look reserved only for little sisters to give to their big brothers.

"Fine. Keep pretending you're going to have a life. I'm going to enjoy what little life I have left before Dad completely ruins it. You'd be a lot less of a butthead if you, you know, did some normal stuff before it's all 'save humanity' this and 'kill the beasts' that! You know, like, girls? Remember them? All 'woo-hoo' and 'mmmmmmmmmauh'?"

She accentuated her ridiculous noises with even more ridiculous girly shakes and air make outs until Ethan finally had enough and threw a pillow at her, which she deflected with impressive speed and agility.

She patted her hair down, obviously trying not to look rattled. "*Fine*. I'm gone! I'm going to the mall! With *people* who don't carry *crossbows*! Have fun marrying your calculus book!"

He had to laugh at her teenage histrionics. But the moment his door slammed shut, Ethan realized his concentration was shot, and of all the things possibly not in his distant future, he knew for a fact the mean value theorem was absolutely not in his immediate future. He shut the book and placed a stack of ancient-looking Latin texts detailing the history of black magic and witches on top. Which was more a metaphor for his life than he wanted to think about.

Charles, their father and the leader of the hunters in the area, was probably in the garage oiling his guns or waxing his bowstrings, no doubt in some stage of glee after forcing Fiona to loose arrows until her fingers callused, punctuating each sharp thwack of arrow meeting target with some fact about wolves, voice rising with each one until he worked himself into a frenzy. Part of Ethan—most of Ethan—knew his father was just this side of batshit insane, but he also knew firsthand the destruction a rogue pack could leave in its wake. So Ethan and his sister followed Charles's every order like the good little soldiers he desired, and only complained to each other in the privacy of their bedrooms.

As was the way of most treaties, not everyone followed the rules. Mostly it meant a quick death, but over the years, certain families, certain packs, became stronger than others and were harder to punish. They were on the fringes for the most part and rarely lasted long before infighting destroyed them or broke them up. But some thrived on the chaos.

One such powerful pack of wolves settled in the South in the eighteen hundreds, having chased down the land boom like so many others. Some of the Robertsons followed them, using the money they obtained both legally and from the corpses of wolves to finance their end of the battles, buying bigger, more effective weapons, learning new ways to kill. Ethan's family became notorious for encouraging treaty-breaking activities, but Ethan still took his destiny, the Robertson destiny, seriously.

But, destiny or no, Ethan actually found archery relaxing. The concentration and skill it required, the burn when he chose not to protect his fingers from the string—sometimes it made him feel better to feel that pain—the breath he forced himself to take just before he let the arrow fly, the satisfying noise it made as it found its target and buried itself, the combination of it all was hypnotic.

He padded his way through the house, careful not to let Charles know he was going out to voluntarily practice hunting skills because he did not want to give him the satisfaction. He strung his bow and slung it across his chest along with his quiver of practice arrows. He thought about heading for the forest. There were squirrels and other small animals that would make for good moving targets, but that was Charles's idea, and Ethan was not a senseless killer.

The university's archery team rarely put away their targets like they were supposed to after practice, and Ethan could usually find the foam and wood blocks shoved by the water fountains near the football practice field. Despite the fact that the targets mysteriously had holes in the bull's-eyes and the team was ranked below last place, no one had yet caught on that someone with actual skill used them from time to time.

Twenty minutes of shooting and it was bull's-eye after bull's-eye, and Ethan was feeling something teetering on the edge of exhilaration, something he would never admit to out loud. Especially in the presence of his father. What was keeping him from falling over the edge was the distinct feeling that someone was watching him.

He could sense it—from behind his left shoulder, about twenty yards back. He focused the bulk of his concentration on the target. The tiny idea of giving his unseen watcher a show made him stand a little straighter, put more into his follow-through. The field was within sight of sorority row, and he wouldn't have put it past some Delta Beta something or other, with less than virtuous intentions, to want to score with a badass-looking archer—especially given the sad state of the "real" archers actually on the team. He was secretly flattered he had an admirer, and if said admirer had a sweet ass and nice breasts and maybe curly red hair if he was really lucky, all the better. Maybe Fi was right about getting a life.

He placed the nock of the arrow on the string and drew back, finding the sweet spot of a full draw where his index finger touched the crook of his mouth. He took a breath and loosed the arrow. It flew true, hitting the foam dead center with a crack, and he smiled to himself.

A slow clap finally broke the spell, and Ethan whipped around, eager to meet the mystery, and, yeah, okay. Not the perky coed he had expected.

"Nice aim." The words were as snarky as they were complimentary, and they originated from a man about Ethan's age with a loose swagger in his step and intelligent blue eyes. "You can't be on the team with aim like that, can you?"

Ethan grinned a little as he straddled his bow across his body, string digging into his chest. "Nah. Just an amateur, really." He slicked his sweaty hair back, confused by how much he was not as disappointed his new fan wasn't a sorority girl as he thought he should have been.

The man rolled his eyes. "Shame. I hear they could use someone who can shoot without shooting himself. Or spectators. Behind him. Or cars down the street. Mind you, I say 'hear' because I'm not about to get shot by one of these morons. I don't come this way when they're here practicing. I was worried until I saw you shoot that first arrow. No one is usually here at this hour, you see, and the sound of an arrow actually hitting a target intrigued me."

The confidence with which he spoke put Ethan on edge just a little. But, no, that wasn't it. It was something else entirely, but he couldn't put his finger on it. And that fact made the edge even thinner.

"Yeah. You, eh, you a big archery fan?" Ethan was keenly aware that more and more little voices in his head were whispering for him to be wary, but he couldn't hone in on why. Charming shouldn't have been a trigger, and he cursed Charles for the thousandth time that day for royally screwing with his expectations of people.

The man looked down almost shyly and then back up slowly and smiled. "Just an amateur fan, really. I was going to cut through the field on my way home when I saw you. I'm quite impressed, I have to say."

"Thanks." Ethan gritted his teeth. "But I really have to get back home myself now. I was just doing this as a break from homework." He retrieved his arrows from the block, never fully turning away from the leather jacket-clad stranger. "Maybe I'll see you around, eh...."

"Liam." He didn't offer a handshake or a head nod, and those eyes hadn't left Ethan, either.

"Okay, Liam. It was nice to—"

"And you are?" But he asked like he already knew. His overconfidence shouldn't have been a trigger either, should it?

Ethan cocked his head to the side. "Ethan, but I really need to—"

"Ethan." Liam seemed to savor the "n," drawing it out a bit. "I'll be seeing you, Ethan, now that I know you sneak over here. It made my trip home so much... more... pleasant, meeting you."

It was only then that Liam extended a hand, and Ethan, because he didn't know what else he should do, took it.

It was warm. Too warm, even for a Florida summer night. Ethan's gaze wandered to where their hands were joined and then up to meet Liam's eyes again. It was something—instinct, training—he didn't have time to figure out which. That close to him, it was so obvious it almost smacked him in the face. All the signs were there. Liam was one of *them*. A wolf. A *Kinnaird*.

Ethan raised an eyebrow and tensed up as he damned himself for giving himself away and for not recognizing all the signs before. And for good measure, he damned Charles for being right.

His bowstring dug into his chest, quiver heavy on his back, and he could have taken him down right there. Even without arrows aimed at the heart and Charles barking orders at him, he could have taken him down, disabled him at the least, but he didn't move.

That monster should have been in pieces by then, not smiling like he had won. His intestines should have been nothing more than fertilizer for the forty yard line. But Ethan pushed the idea down deep because it wasn't his, it was Charles's. He looked for a reason to strike, but the truth of it all was that Liam had not given him a reason to. He was not attacking. He was not even threatening to attack. And Ethan respected the rules, even if Charles rarely did so himself.

More than that, Ethan was intrigued.

Ethan bit his lip and kept eye contact, and the moment he regretted most when he replayed the scene in his head later that night was not how he just stood there when he should have been doing *something*, but how he flinched like a scared rabbit as Liam leaned in close, hot and smelling of earth and leaves and a lingering, sharp tang of blood.

"I'm going now, Ethan. Going home. You're not going to use that bow on me because if you do, you won't see me again. You don't want that, do you?" Liam paused, his eyes half-closed. He backed away from Ethan a few inches, and it brought Liam's features into sharp focus. "Ohhhhh. You *don't* want that. I can hear your heartbeat, Ethan. I have since you stepped onto the field. Your heart is racing as fast as it does when you make a shot, and that's not fear I smell on you."

Liam leaned in again, this time to inhale deeply at the base of Ethan's neck. And this time Ethan didn't flinch. Liam let out the breath, and hot air rushed against Ethan's sweaty skin, and it was possibly the most erotic moment in his recent memory.

"No. Fear has a *very* different scent than what I am getting right now. But I don't have to tell you that. I'm pretty sure you're very aware of your current... situation." Liam fell back and took a little bow. "Go home, Ethan. Finish your work. I'll be around, I can promise you." He turned, confident, fearless, knowing Ethan would do nothing more than stand there until he disappeared into the tree line on the other side of the field.

And Ethan did exactly that. Those little voices were now screaming at him, in Charles's voice no less, to run him through and parade his corpse through the city, but he stood there, willing both his heartbeat and erection to calm.

Through the imaginary din of generations of Robertsons past expressing profound disappointment, he heard a voice of reason, his own, telling himself how well and truly fucked he really was.

CHAPTER 2

HE DIDN'T see Liam the next day. Not physically, at least. If he saw him in his mind later on that same night as he stroked himself in the shower, well, Ethan chalked that up to some lingering effect of what was most definitely the supernatural power of the first ever known werewolf curse. It was, he told himself over and over, absolutely not a natural result of their highly charged encounter on the field.

He didn't tell Charles either. Or Fi. He might not have liked Charles all too much, but he didn't want to be disowned, or worse, punished for letting Liam live.

He also definitely didn't go out of his way to run into Liam again, and if he found himself taking ridiculously out-of-the-way routes home through the practice fields and the forest behind it, then it was obviously for the exercise.

Three days passed, and all he had to show for his efforts was a halfhearted apology letter from the archery head coach from when he almost took an arrow to the shin walking on the other side of the fence behind the archers (*They are getting better, I swear, but please consider walking on the other side of the street and carrying a shield of some sort if you have to come within 150 feet of the archery fields for now.*) and several new fantasies he found himself indulging in more and more.

He had been ignoring Charles's demands to train, citing his heavy course load as an excuse, but Saturday came and Charles dragged him and Fiona to the forest with a small arsenal, and no excuse would cut it.

They set up in a large clearing tucked away from where normal people were usually allowed. Because Charles owned one of the largest hunting, camping, and fishing outfitters in the tri-county area and supplied the city's government employees with discount ammo, weapons, and fishing supplies, both public and personal, he was allowed to venture far off the public path. The clearing was perfect, even Ethan had to admit it. Several downed trees and cracked stumps became resting places for small targets, and the town council looked the other way when raccoons and other pest populations were thinned out slightly.

Fiona was on fire. Most girls her age could barely lift some of the larger assault weapons, but Fiona wielded them as if they were weightless. Nearly every shot found its mark, even with Charles's distracting fire-and-brimstone sermons. Ethan was content working on distance aiming, setting up his shots 100 or more yards away. While Fi was always an in-your-face kind of girl, he was perfectly happy from a distance, watching the scene before he made an entrance. He supposed it was a good trait for a sniper. That and a disturbing lack of desire to get his hands dirty.

Charles was at the point in his speech where he started to damn the wolves as abominations against God and nature, and Ethan could make it out even from that much of a distance. He shifted uncomfortably on the wet ground, underbrush poking into his belly. He almost wanted to aim for one of Fiona's targets just to get Charles to stop talking, even for a minute, but as soon as he lowered his eye to the scope, he got that familiar prickly shiver that told him they were not alone in the forest.

The distant snap of a twig from about ten yards back confirmed his suspicions, but he stayed on his own target and squeezed off the last shot of the round, effectively leaving him unarmed. He stood and turned toward the sound, but the dense pine and oak did not afford him the best view. He bent back down to lock the safety and left the edge of the clearing to venture deeper into the forest.

He did not have to walk far before he heard it—the smooth, snarky tone and now familiar voice-over of his new and very explicit fantasies. "Looking for me?"

Ethan whipped around to find Liam leaning against a tree as if he owned the goddamned forest. He put on his best nonchalant face, which of course was going to fool absolutely no one.

"I thought it might be a bear." Immediate and total regret washed over him. Stupid answers were beneath him. He was twenty years old, damn it.

Liam moved like a cheetah, and he was inches away from Ethan in the span of a breath. "Now, now. Ethan. Ignoring the fact that I can hear your heart and smell your hormones, why would you go after a bear unarmed?"

"I—I wasn't looking for you, I...." Stammering was also beneath him. How could he let this guy—this *wolf*—do this to him?

Liam looked amused. "Come on, Ethan. You think I haven't seen you all week? Walking twice a day through the field where we met? Taking wild detours through the forests? You've been looking for me. And here I am. And you left your weapon behind. I'm flattered, Ethan, really."

"You've been following me?" His chest was tight, but it was not from embarrassment as much as it was from anticipation.

"Yes." No lies. No stammering around the truth. Liam was unapologetic.

"All this week? Everywhere?" Ethan blushed at the thought of what Liam might have seen in that week.

Liam snorted. "Now, Ethan. I do have a life." He leaned in close to Ethan's ear, and Ethan silently blamed the heat coming off Liam reacting with his cold sweat for the long shiver. "But I've followed you enough. Tell me, are you thinking of me when you're alone in your bedroom? God, I hope so, because that face you make when you come, I'd really like to see that face when you're under me. I'd like to make you come myself instead of watching you think of me from a distance." He backed up, blinked slowly, and watched Ethan for a reaction.

Ethan tried to shake the fog of confusion and arousal, and he opened his mouth to speak, but not before he heard Fiona in the distance yelling for him.

Shit.

Liam rolled his eyes and sighed. "I guess that's my cue, isn't it, Ethan? Can't have Daddy and little sister knowing about our little secret, can we?" He turned to leave but stopped short. "Still, it isn't fair leaving you this way." Liam smirked and raised an eyebrow as he surveyed Ethan. "No, you need something new to think about tonight."

And before Ethan knew what was happening, Liam's lips were on his. It was hot—literally and figuratively—and Liam's lips were soft and tasted of the same earthy tang Liam smelled of on the day they'd met. Ethan relaxed into it faster than he liked, and he let Liam's tongue explore his own. He didn't need Liam to tell him his heart was racing. He could feel it kick against his rib cage, and it served to spur Liam on. Liam's hands wrapped around the back of Ethan's neck, and Ethan lifted his jaw slightly so Liam could kiss his way down to a spot Ethan's shirt barely hid. Liam didn't bite hard enough to break the skin, but there was certainly going to be a mark, more so because Ethan jerked up into it. He didn't even care about how weak it made him seem or the noise that escaped when he felt sharp teeth.

Liam came away smiling and admired his masterpiece: red and purple and, in a few minutes from then, in dire need of a quick explanation from Ethan if he couldn't find a way to cover it up. While Ethan adjusted his shirt as best he could, Liam disappeared beyond the tree line. Fiona was still calling for him, and Charles had joined in by that point. Their voices grew more worried with every yell. Ethan was in the frustrating predicament of thinking up an excuse for his absence, so willing his erection down, at least at that moment, was easy. But he knew as soon as he was alone again, he would come harder than ever, thinking of Liam's soft lips and knowing eyes watching him that night.

Yep. He was totally and completely screwed.

CHAPTER 3

ETHAN MADE his way back to the clearing eventually with, he hoped, no signs of an illicit make out. Once he was done yelling at Ethan, Charles inspected their targets while Fiona dismantled one of the rifles. She looked at him strangely for a second, eyes sweeping up and down.

"You okay there, big brother? You look a little… spooked."

Women.

He played it off with a grin. "Yeah, Fi. I just thought I heard something back in the woods. Wanted to check it out."

She raised an eyebrow after another generous five-second pause. "And?"

"Nothing. Squirrel, maybe." He joined her in dismantling the guns, but turned away slightly to hide the mark that was definitely not going away any time soon.

"Really, Ethan? 'Cause you were gone a long time." She was not going to give it up. Because she was a little sister. Because she was Fiona. Because she was a Robertson.

Ethan sighed. "Big squirrel. Now, hand me that case over there, Fi. I have a chemistry test on Monday I have to study for."

She pursed her lips, and he knew that look meant they would be revisiting the subject in the future, but Charles had made his way back over with his targets, and she might have been be a brat, but even she wouldn't go that far to involve him.

"Not bad, son. Not bad at all. You're still aiming a bit low, but as long as that bullet pierces the flesh and the silver poisons his blood, he'll be dead anyway. In fact, not getting his heart means he'll suffer more before he goes."

Ethan's stomach actually turned at the sight of his father's gleeful face.

Fiona crossed her eyes, puffed her cheeks out, and blew in annoyance. Both Robertson children were pretty sure the trees could recite all his motivational speeches by then.

"What do you say, kids? I have twenty boxes of bullets in the garage that need to be infused with poison."

Fi shot up. "Daaaaaaad. Come on! It's Saturday. I've already promised Susan I'd go to the beach with her." She jutted out her lower lip in a pretty impressive pout. "You can't make me do this stuff 24/7, Dad! I'm fifteen!"

Charles turned to his son, but Ethan cut him off before he could speak. "Nope. No, Dad. I have a test to study for. You promised you wouldn't interfere with my schoolwork if I dedicated twenty hours a week to training. I'm holding up my end."

Charles sighed. "Fine. This time." Both Ethan and Fiona knew that tone of voice meant there would be three times as much work waiting for them when they got home, but neither could muster up the care.

Fiona punched a fist up in victory and smiled at her brother. "And you have to take me to Susan's. Her dad gets really nervous when Dad shows up with all those guns in the back of the truck." Double victory. He could see it on her face.

"All right, brat." He rolled his eyes in defeat.

Ethan and Fiona helped load the guns and ammo into Charles's truck, and Fiona raced Ethan to his car. She started before he even buckled in.

"You're a big, fat liar, by the way. Squirrel. Really? I hope you're ready for rabies shots, because that 'squirrel' looks dangerous." She reached over and pulled at the collar of his shirt to reveal the mark. "You met up with someone in the woods. Who was she? Obviously someone special if you couldn't be without her for one morning. You do know how stupid it was to have her come so close to the clearing, right? Or are you just stupid in love? I want to meet her, Ethan. I want to meet the girl who made you stupider."

If she weren't his sister, he would have sped up and shoved her out the door. He turned on the "annoyed big brother" voice. "*It's no one*, Fi. Mind your own business!"

She looked overdramatically taken aback and clutched her chest. "Oh. *My*. She *is* someone special. Is she the one, Ethan? Are you going *to marry* her and have, like, a thousand ugly little babies? I'm going to have to sneak behind your boring backs and teach them how to be awesome, aren't I? Aunt Fiona. The cool aunt. Yeah." She reclined a little in her seat and clasped her hands behind her head.

He actually tried to will the passenger door to open magically so she would fall out. "Fi. Shut. Up."

Fiona knew the tone. "All right, all right! Geez! All I'm saying is that I want to meet her. Sheesh. What has your panties in a twist today?"

He made a sharp turn up Susan's road. "Look, Fi. No offense, but Dad is trying to take over my life right now and school is hellish enough already without his insane training demands. If I want to keep my scholarship, I have to keep my GPA up. I barely have time to study, and every time I try to, he tries to find some excuse why I shouldn't. So, please, darling sister, let me have something in my life that is just mine, okay? No Dad. No too-curious little sister. No guns, no bows, no mystical… things." He waved his hand all around because, God, it seemed the supernatural was everywhere.

She looked down at her beach bag, filled with her bikini and towel and sunscreen and… normality. And she softened. She reached over and ruffled his hair a bit. "Okay, Ethan. Sorry."

He smiled, despite the lie he'd told his own sister. Nothing, *nothing* was normal about this. He pulled up to Susan's house, and Fi bounced out in a sudden flurry of teenage energy. He watched her go and knew that if she were in his position, he would dismember Liam for messing with his family. Fi would do the same if she knew. Hell, she would probably do worse and laugh for days afterward. She might only be fifteen and had just disappeared into a group of giggling, dancing girls, but Ethan saw the sharp edges of a sadistic streak in his baby sister. And he feared for the person who would eventually bring that boiling to the surface.

He wasn't lying. He did have a chemistry test to study for, but as soon as he got home, he found himself shirtless and staring at the mark in the mirror. He touched it lightly, feeling phantom lips and hearing a ghostly snark of "*I knew you wanted something new to think about.*"

He wondered if Liam was watching him right then, watching him caress the spot where his mouth had been, and this wasn't showing off in archery or target shooting. This was real and dangerous and intimate.

He shed his jeans and pretended it was because they were too dirty from the forest. Like he was not going to acknowledge the very real possibility that Liam was lurking, spying, waiting for him. He placed them in the hamper deliberately and still tried to keep up the appearance that nothing but a shower would follow. His boxers were next, and it wouldn't have taken supercharged, supernatural sight, even at a distance, to see that he was very hard.

His cock jerked a bit when he touched the mark again and he tried in quiet desperation to use it to connect, to tie himself to Liam. His free hand slid downward to grasp his erection, and he turned to face the window so anyone who might have been hiding in the trees would have the best view. He pumped slowly, savored every sensation, watched every stroke deliberately, and hoped Liam was out there doing the same. He pulled and twisted slightly at the end, just as he liked it, and voyeur watching or not, Ethan was not going to settle for anything less than a stellar orgasm.

He tried to hold out, tried to go as long as he could. He stroked himself long and slow, teased out his orgasm to drive Liam mad. But the thoughts of Liam watching, watching just how he was affecting Ethan, maybe even touching himself as he watched… he was almost embarrassed by how quickly the feeling built and curled up from down low as a hot flush worked its way downward. He breathed in quick, shallow hitches and bit his lip, and he knew he had to be a sight. He stroked the bite mark and wondered how those lips would feel all over him as they nipped, sucked, and licked Ethan.

In his mind he and Liam were on the forest floor, naked, and Liam was howling, gnashing his teeth, primal and wild, as Ethan took everything Liam gave him, and it was this fantasy that drove him over the edge as his strokes sped up beyond his control. He tensed, back arched and eyes screwed shut, and he should have moaned or shouted or grunted, but madness overtook him and he whispered but one word as thick ropes covered his hand. "Liam."

CHAPTER 4

ETHAN GAVE Fiona credit. She'd kept her word to stay mum on what she thought was a college girlfriend situation. Although, it was Fiona, so he had to do her chores and chauffeur her around, and he had to take her insults and mocking without retaliation. The first time he even looked like he was going to protest, she fingered the collar of her shirt innocently, reminding him in one sweet, doe-eyed, hair-flippy move that she could wrestle him to the ground and point out the slowly fading hickey to Charles to start a barrage of questions.

Ethan couldn't sleep. He had been lying in bed for hours by then, and he watched the clock tick away the precious little time left until he had to get up for class. He wasn't able to sneak away to run by the field and forest at any point during the day, and memorizing formulas took up the bulk of the evening. He didn't know if atomic ground states running through his head like an annoying pop song were keeping him up or if it was the disturbing addiction to Liam he seemed to have developed. He couldn't even rationalize his feelings toward a supposed enemy who was apparently stalking him. A werewolf. A creature he was born and bred to destroy.

He should have been, according to Charles, delighting in imagining Liam's blood painting the forest floor, Liam's flesh ripped open. and the light draining from his eyes as he suffered in death. But Ethan couldn't shake the image of the two of them, naked and intertwined in the moonlight, Liam's eyes glowing brighter the more aroused Ethan made him.

It had been just shy of thirty-six hours since their encounter in the forest. He tossed and turned the rest of the night, maybe managing an hour of decent sleep. Closing his eyes meant seeing Liam, and sleeping meant seeing Liam in his dreams when he needed to be dreaming of covalent bonds. Sometime between 5:00 a.m. and sunrise, he decided this was all Liam's fault and reluctantly headed off to take a long, cold shower.

Coffee was a godsend to his addled brain, but offered nothing in the way of curing the dark circles under his eyes. Even Fiona looked sorry for him as he poured a second cup. And a third. He threw on jeans and plaid shirt and let gravity decide what his hair would do before he stumbled out the door into the harsh summer morning sun. He had no idea how passing a chemistry test was even possible in his current state, much less acing it.

He pulled into a parking spot thankfully close to the science building and sat in his car, rolling his head to work out the kinks in his neck as he silently pictured the structures of atoms. After five minutes, he gathered his things and prepared for the worst.

He concentrated on the sound of his shoes on the loose gravel. Lost in the rhythm of step—*atomic weight*—step—*atomic number*, he made his way to the door, but stopped short when he caught a glimpse of a dark figure in his peripheral vision. He focused through the haze of sunshine and exhaustion, and there was Liam, staring at him as if he had every right to. He wore dark jeans and a black shirt and looked every bit the dangerous man he was.

Ethan stared back but didn't change direction to go to him and didn't wonder why he was there. He silently cursed Liam for his sleepless night, and he knew, *he knew*, Liam could see his red and puffy eyes and sleep-deprived pale skin from across the quad, and Ethan wanted him to know that Liam alone was responsible for them. He tried to make an angry face, but Liam was unwavering and his stare was so intense Ethan could practically feel it like a physical touch.

Ethan was frozen. Class started in five minutes. He licked his too-dry lips, and he was breathing too heavily for not having moved, and he knew Liam could see that as well. Ethan became faintly aware of steps behind him, and a hand on his shoulder broke the spell.

"Dude, you okay? You look like shit, man." It was a voice so stupidly happy and confident that it could only be Kevin Hughes, an insufferable know-it-all Ethan had known since he was a kid. Being raised in an old and powerful Wiccan family only helped in chemistry, and Kevin had the dubious honor of setting the curve in the class. Ethan blinked and shook his head to clear the fog.

The Hughes family was allies, and Kevin, unlike Ethan, was fiercely loyal to the cause and an insufferable suck-up. If he caught wind of Liam, Kevin would run to Charles without hesitation.

Ethan smiled forcefully. "What? Oh, yeah. Fine, fine. Just—just up late last night studying. Going over things in my head last minute. How about you? Ready for this?" He knew if he got Kevin talking, he'd be too distracted to notice Liam standing there like he wanted to fuck Ethan against the side of the building. They walked in unison up the steps and, as Kevin babbled on about the test and how his five-year-old sister could pass it, Ethan afforded himself one look back before opening the door.

Liam was gone.

THE SUN had set hours before, and it was still hot even with the AC running, so Ethan let the sounds of Peter Murphy drift out the window he had left open to invite in any cool breeze that might happen to come his way. It was too hot to concentrate on studying for his trig test, and he knew he was no good like this, but something had to occupy the space in his mind that so desperately wanted to be filled with Liam.

His brain told him *arcsin, arctan, arccosec*, but his dick argued back with *Liam, Liam, Liam*, and he damned Liam for his constant distractions.

He pushed open his shirt a little, unbuttoned a button to see the faint outline of the mark still fading away, but he shook his head to clear it a bit and vowed to get back to studying. Which lasted all of three seconds before the situation in his jeans grew too urgent to ignore.

"Ah, fuck it." He shut his trig book and slammed the pencil down on his desk. It was no use, and with an erection that refused to go down no matter how many times he repeated Heron's Law in his head, it was a great effort to have the coordination to get up and lock his door so Fi or Charles wouldn't barge in, even at the late hour.

Five minutes. He would give himself five minutes to indulge himself a bit, and then it was right back to studying. He threw off his overshirt and sat on his bed. He unbuttoned his jeans as he stretched across the bedspread. He slid a hand in and took himself in a loose grip before shoving down his jeans and boxers a little as he lifted his hips. He teased himself for a few moments, thrusting into his fist and scratching at his skin like he wanted Liam to do—never enough to break the skin, but enough to hurt and to hint at the threat Liam could be if he wanted to be.

It was his excitement at the danger of this whole thing that should have scared him and not thrilled him as much as it did.

He took a break to slick himself up, do it up right, and he was lost in his fantasies almost immediately again. This one, the one he went to more and more these days, was a particularly erotic vision of him and Liam, deep in the forest, running naked and free, fucking on the forest floor, up against a tree, wild and loud with no one around to hear them cry out but each other. He closed his eyes and stroked faster as he listened to the sounds of flesh on wet flesh and his breath sped up, getting shallower with every stroke.

It was so good he almost missed the bed shake at its foot a bit. Like someone had joined him. His eyes flew open, and before he could focus on the dark shape sitting there, Liam lunged forward and straddled him.

"Thinking of me, Ethan?" There was a smirk on his face. An affectionate smirk, but a smirk nonetheless. Ethan released himself to cover up, to reach for Liam, but Liam grabbed his hands and pushed them back down. "Don't stop."

Ethan raised an eyebrow, but Liam just grinned and leaned in close.

"Wanna watch, Ethan. I can't watch you from outside tonight. I can smell you. I can hear you whisper my name when you come. It's making me *crazy*. I don't care that it's not the middle of the night and no one else is asleep. I'll leave as soon as you're done, I promise. Please, Ethan."

The pleading desperation in his blue eyes was not something Ethan was prepared to say no to. The arousal at the confirmation that Liam had watched that night after the forest was not something he could even try to refuse.

"Okay, okay. But, Liam, you have to be quiet. Charles is just down the hall. And Fi too." Ethan relaxed a tiny bit.

Liam's smile was shy, his words anything but. "I could hear your heartbeat when you saw me this morning. Do you know how hot it is to know how much I'm affecting you this way? I wanted to fuck you up against the building right then. Might have done it too if it weren't for your friend." Liam leaned in and kissed him, soft and promising, with none of the anxiety that should come with sneaking into a hunter's home and seducing his son.

They didn't break contact when Liam pulled them both to a sitting position and Ethan rested against the wall behind him. Liam deepened the kisses and wrapped his hand around Ethan's, guiding it gently back to his cock, and Ethan dutifully picked up the rhythm again. Having Liam there made the feeling so much better, he couldn't help but groan into his mouth, and it earned him an amused "sssshhhhh" from Liam against his lips.

Their shirts came off, and it was skin on skin. Ethan didn't mind the sticky sweat between them, an unavoidable side effect of the Florida heat, and Liam wrapped his legs around Ethan and leaned back a bit so he could see what Ethan was doing to himself. It made Ethan stroke faster when he saw Liam couldn't tear his eyes away from it, made him moan and gasp when he felt Liam grind into him as best he could in that position, and silence fast became an impossible option. Liam tried to swallow his noises for him, to take him in and distract him, but Ethan was overloaded with sensation and losing control. Not even the threat of Charles barging in and catching them could keep him quiet.

Liam must have sensed or heard something Ethan couldn't, because his blue eyes went wide and he clamped his hand over Ethan's mouth and held it there.

"Your sister's in the hallway," he mouthed, and Ethan stopped moving altogether, stopped even breathing, and for a moment, it was nothing but crickets outside and "Indigo Eyes" coming from his stereo.

When Liam visibly relaxed, Ethan wondered if the spell was broken and he would have to finish alone—and he needed to finish *right then*. He had stopped twice, and it was making him frustrated and desperate and that much more horny. Liam lifted himself off Ethan's lap and stood on the floor next to the bed. Ethan frowned.

"But—"

Before he could finish, Liam placed a finger to Ethan's lips and smiled. He quietly took off his own jeans and boxers and left them in a heap as he rejoined Ethan on the bed, this time pushing him down and stretching himself out over Ethan, kissing him and encouraging his hips to lift up so he could push his bottoms off the rest of the way.

"You're getting off on this, aren't you, Liam? We could be caught at any minute, and you just made it that much harder to hide." Ethan thanked God he was so close to Liam he could watch the goose bumps rise as he whispered against Liam's skin.

Liam didn't answer, but lined himself up perfectly with Ethan, bringing himself down so their dicks touched. Before Ethan could cry out at that new sensation, Liam's hand found his mouth again while he continued to grind down, slicking both of them up with precome and sweat and leftover lube still coating Ethan as he moved. Ethan felt like he could die right then from the feeling, but his desire to just *come already* kept him going.

"Are you going to be quiet now, Ethan?"

Lying never got anyone anywhere. He shook his head. If Liam let go, he might sing his orgasm from the rooftops.

Liam shrugged innocently and sat up. He pulled Ethan up to sitting as well and kept his hand on his mouth. Liam reached between them and took them both in his other hand, pumping slowly at first, staring at Ethan to gauge his reaction. Ethan whimpered quietly and closed his eyes, breathing hot on Liam's hand, but didn't try to shove it away.

Liam sped up, and the contrast between rough palm and velvet softness of his cock was intense. Every nerve was on fire, and Ethan's skin tingled from his head all the way down. He could hear the slick sounds, his own hitched breathing just under the music, and even with the danger just outside his door and the open window to the world, these noises were just for them. Liam's uneven breaths were just for him, and his own quiet moans from behind Liam's hands were just for Liam. And it was this thought of *belonging* that fired right to his core.

He opened his eyes. Liam was still watching him, and then— *fuck*—he came hard, struggling to keep quiet and spilling over Liam's hand, which Liam then used to slick them up more. Soon Liam was coming as well. He never broke eye contact as his mouth parted and his body tightened against Ethan. Liam was beautiful when he came.

They kissed as they came down, trying to slow their breathing together. It was intimate in a way he had never felt before, and Liam traced a hand along his skin, adding to the sensation of cooling, drying sweat and come that made him shiver, and the tremendous muscle release all over his body made him shake slightly too. *I probably look like a mess.* But Liam kept touching him and kept letting Ethan touch him, and Ethan finally calmed down, finally breathed normally again.

"That was...." Fuck. There was no way to describe when they were together. *Hot. Crazy. Amazing. Dangerous. Addictive. Wrong.*

Liam smiled. "Yeah. It was." He slid off Ethan's lap and stood to search for his clothing.

Ethan could only watch with something damned close to possessiveness as Liam bent over to pull on his jeans. Liam caught him staring and lunged at him, capturing his mouth in a heated kiss, like he didn't want it to be over yet, but he regained some semblance of control and pulled away again to put on his shirt.

Ethan's heart stopped for a moment when there was a knock at the door. *Shit.* Charles.

"Umm... just a second!"

Liam grinned at Ethan, still naked and scrambling around for his clothes. He grabbed Ethan for a final kiss and a whispered promise of more when it was safe again and disappeared out the open window.

"Ethan, is everything okay in there? I thought I heard—"

"Everything's fine! Just studying." He managed his jeans, at least. He hopped up and down to get them on faster and cursed the noise Charles could surely hear.

"Are you sure? Because I—"

Ethan flung open the door breathlessly. "Everything's good, thanks."

Charles didn't look quite convinced. "All right, then, but Ethan, I expect you to help me build traps tomorrow afternoon after school. No excuses."

"Yes. Okay. No problem. I'll be there." No one gets breathless from studying, damn it. *Calm down.* He smiled, as if it made him look more trustworthy.

Charles peered past him into his room, eyed the open window a bit too long. *So screwed.* "See that you are." Charles raised his eyebrow and started to walk away.

Ethan closed the door and leaned against it in some kind of relieved anxiety, if that could even be a thing. He heard Charles knock on Fi's door next, and he listened through the wall as Charles made the same demand on her for the next afternoon, but before he left Fiona, Ethan heard one last demand—for information.

"Fiona, does your brother have a girlfriend I don't know about?"

Ethan recalled the conversation in his car about letting him have something that was just his, and he was now, more than ever, glad his bratty baby sister didn't listen to a word he said.

"*Totally*, Dad. He made me swear I wouldn't tell anyone, but he's got a secret girlfriend he doesn't want anyone to know about because he's all *embarrassed* about the hunting stuff and, like, probably us too."

"Now, Fiona. Your brother has a good head on his shoulders, and this must be a special lady he doesn't want to scare off. He'll tell her in his own time, I know it. Besides, we don't want too many people knowing about us and what we do until we know they are ready to join us in the fight. He's doing the right thing, not telling her yet. But I don't know why he wouldn't tell us. I can be—"

"No, Dad, you can't!" He could hear her giggle mockingly. "You can't be normal about anything. Look at how many of my friends won't come over to the house anymore! And don't you dare tell Ethan I told you this! I'll *die*."

The conversation continued and changed subjects, and he breathed a sigh of actual relief. He went to his window and caught a glimpse of Liam sitting in the tree just outside. He smiled at Ethan. They were safe. For now.

"Jesus. What the hell am I doing?" he said, not in anger or frustration or disappointment, just a general observation of his life at that moment.

He waited until morning to discreetly make his way to the washer with his sheets and went downstairs for some breakfast.

CHAPTER 5

IT BECAME a thing, this… whatever it was. Ethan never knew when Liam would pop up.

Sometimes it was after class, staring at him from across the parking lot. Sometimes it was in the dead of night, while he slept. Sometimes Ethan went for long drives way out of town just to see how far Liam would follow him, and without fail, Liam always found him.

The common denominator was that, within minutes, they were on each other, kissing like it might be the last time they'd ever get the chance. Their hands roamed beneath layers of leather and cotton, and it felt so good, and yet it felt so wrong. He was trained better than this, damn it. He should have said no. Needed to say stop. But he didn't want to. Especially not when Liam was on top of him, rutting against him so they both came on each other, Liam's hand over his mouth if they were in his bedroom.

Ethan parked on the edge of Green Swamp, a few miles out of town, his initial embarrassment at parking like teenagers to make out fading quickly. Liam interrupted a kiss to slide out of the car and came around to the driver's side to pull Ethan out as well. Liam tugged on his arms, and Ethan stood, slightly confused, but Liam pulled him close. He felt Liam's heat in sharp contrast with the slightly chill night, and Liam closed the door behind them.

"All caged up in there." He shrugged off his shirt. "I'm an animal, Ethan. Gotta be free." He lifted Ethan's shirt, and Ethan let him take it completely off.

"Doesn't this feel better? The air on your skin? The creatures in the forest watching us? Look at yourself in the moonlight. Look how it dances on your skin as the trees move. *Gorgeous*. If I could convince you to be with me all the time, I would. We'd run free, Ethan. You and me. Taking everything we wanted and fucking in the wild." He reached for Ethan's jeans, but Ethan grabbed his hand and stopped him.

"Liam, are you trying to turn me?"

Liam looked bemused. "And lose my human? No, Ethan. Your humanity is a major part of what makes you so attractive, even if you would be an amazing wolf. It's just so hot watching you struggle to justify me to yourself."

Ethan still hadn't let go. "So, I'm a challenge for you to overcome."

Liam raised an eyebrow in silent exasperation. "Ethan. If I wanted a challenge, I would have made it challenging. You submitted pretty quickly to me and I'm still here. I don't think I could stop now even if I wanted to. It's becoming something akin to an addiction, my feelings toward you."

Ethan knew Liam could hear his heart pounding at Liam's directness.

"And, frankly, I need my fix." Liam flexed his wrist to remind Ethan, just in case he hadn't figured it out, that it was time to let go.

Liam removed his own jeans and shoes and stood before Ethan completely naked and free. He looked like a wild creature as he pushed Ethan back against the side of the car. He fell to the ground, knees hitting the soft, wet earth, and went again for the rest of Ethan's clothing. This time Ethan didn't stop him.

The night air hit his erection like electricity, and before he could protest the cold, Liam reached out and kept his dick warm in his hands. Ethan looked down at Liam, and he knew what was happening. They had not gone that far yet, and the fantasy of what Liam's mouth would feel like on him, teeth bared but so, so careful, had kept him awake for far too many hours. Now he could finally, *finally* get to see if the expectation held up to the reality.

Liam didn't tease. He didn't hesitate. His unapologetic ways extended to sex, and Liam was swallowing Ethan down before he could steady himself, and it was so, so much better than Ethan had ever fantasized. Liam didn't just put his mouth into it. He put his whole body into pleasuring Ethan.

His tongue swirled around the head, and any attempts to thrust or jerk his hips were thwarted by supernaturally strong hands. The sharp bite on his skin only made him harder, and Ethan wondered if this was a kink or just Liam.

Liam scooted forward and wrapped his lower half around Ethan's leg, grinding against him to relieve some of the agony of his own erection. Ethan could only imagine the sight they made together. He reached down and ran his fingers through Liam's hair, encouraging him to go as far as he wanted.

Liam hollowed his cheeks, wrapped his mouth completely around him, and it was clear he was not looking for a slow burn that night. He sped up, lips swollen, slick, and glistening in the moonlight, and being naked in the forest was a thousand times more erotic, just like Liam had said it would be.

Liam snaked around and massaged Ethan's ass, feeling around as the muscles tightened. Ethan felt the low moans and grunts around his cock, and it was too much, just all too much, and he grabbed at Liam's shoulders, trying to warn him. Liam just pulled himself closer still and brought one hand back round to gently cup Ethan's balls just at the right moment to send him falling, flying, over the edge. Ethan was loud, louder than he meant to be, but he was free like Liam and he felt like a wild creature too, and Liam didn't recoil or spit like the girls he had dated in the past did. He took everything Ethan had, and Liam was so responsive he didn't have to guess whether he was enjoying himself.

When Ethan could breathe normally again, Liam released him gently, letting him fall out of his mouth. Liam rustled the leaves and twigs as he tried to stand, but Ethan pushed him back down, not caring about the dirt or the sharp stones and wood that littered the ground. Ethan fell with him, not wanting him to get away before he returned the favor. He needed to taste Liam like Liam had tasted him.

Liam rested on his elbows, watching Ethan's every move. He hovered over Liam, daring him to try to get away. This was his, damn it.

He started at Liam's neck, inhaling as Liam always did, and the mere implication that Ethan seemed to be scenting him caused Liam's head to fall back. He moved down and bit at Liam's chest, tasting the tang he had come to know as simply Liam. He found a nipple and bit a little harder, and Liam whined and tried to jerk up, but Ethan held him steady. It was for show, for Ethan's benefit, and they both knew it. Liam could have thrown him across the forest with a finger if he wanted to. The real thing that held him down was his *want*.

He continued biting all the way down and eventually settled between Liam's legs, scraping his fingernails down Liam's side as he did. The welts rose and turned red, and Ethan knew they shouldn't have lasted as long as they did. Liam must have liked the way Ethan couldn't stop looking at them. He must have not been bothering with the energy needed to heal them. Ethan grasped Liam's cock and angled it so he could take it in his mouth. He lowered his head and inhaled around the base, letting Liam see what he was doing. Liam groaned a long "Ooooooohhhhhh," and Ethan seized the moment and slipped Liam's cock between his lips.

Liam bit off the end of his moan with a choked noise. Ethan took in as much as he could. He didn't have supernatural strength or a supernatural gag reflex, but he hoped his enthusiasm more than made up for that. He sucked in earnest, using his tongue and his hands to help. He tasted bitter drops in his mouth, and Liam was squirming, his hand holding Ethan's head, guiding it to a perfect rhythm. He felt Liam's legs tense around him and his toes curl into him. It was the only warning he got before Liam cried out, howled, and Ethan's mouth filled with more and more. He tried to swallow as fast as it came, but just as secretly dating a wolf was new to him, so was going down on someone. He felt Liam spasm and twitch, and the look on his face told Ethan he didn't care that Ethan wasn't an expert at it. Liam was beautiful when he came. He was everything Ethan had imagined, and maybe he could call Liam an addiction too.

They stayed on the forest floor for a long time, kissing and touching each other, until they heard howls in the distance.

Liam sat up and looked alarmed. "Ethan, you'd better go." He stood up and threw Ethan his clothes.

"Is it your family?" Ethan pulled up his jeans and slid his shirt over his head quickly.

"Yes. And they don't sound happy." Liam left his own clothing on the ground. Obviously he didn't need them. Ethan suddenly realized he had never seen Liam turn before and wondered if now was his chance. "I have to go now. Don't wait for me. Go home." He pushed Ethan against the car one last time for a searing kiss and turned away. "Ethan, go now. Get in your car and drive and don't look back. Do this for me."

Something in Liam's voice told him not to disobey. Ethan found his keys in his pocket and, once he was in the driver's seat, started the car. He threw the transmission into reverse and turned toward the forest's exit. Driving away, he heard the howls and whoops grow louder, like a macabre overture to something Ethan felt like he should have been fighting against.

CHAPTER 6

CHARLES GOT the call the next morning from a contact at the coroner's office. A man, an ally, a hunter was dead. Four more were in the hospital with varying injuries.

The official cause was a vicious animal attack, coyotes or panthers, but the grim photographs Charles hung on the wall of his office later that day showed the obvious to a trained eye, signs of something more intelligent, more *ritualistic*.

Alan left behind a wife and three children. The quiet rage Ethan watched bloom across his father's face was terrifying. Before he could stop to think, to really wonder if Liam had blood on his hands and what that would mean, the house filled with men and women hell-bent on revenge, armed to the teeth, each new arrival with a more devastating weapon than the last.

Charles was in full military general mode—barking orders, laying out maps and diagrams—and his plans included Ethan fighting, taking out men, women, and children. His plan was indiscriminate.

Charles was adamant. They formed a plan to attack. That night. And getting away to warn Liam was not an option with all the hunters gathered.

Charles set him to work with Fi and a few of the other younger members of the group. It was grunt work, infusing bullets with the right combinations of plant extracts and powdered metals. The rich, loamy soil of the swamp was perfect for growing secret crops of poisonous herbs, and Charles's knowledge of the perfect infusions to cause maximum damage and pain were envied across the South. There was an air of crude sophistication to the method, but it worked.

Ethan prayed such a bullet would not leave his shotgun that night.

Darkness fell more quickly than Ethan liked, and after a lengthy fire-and-brimstone sermon from Charles, the group split off into several pickup trucks and headed to the forest. Charles led the way with a gleeful Fiona in the backseat and Ethan nervously clutching the roll bar as his father tore through to the clearing where Liam had first kissed him.

It didn't take long to find the pack. They also had wounded, and that indicated to Ethan that it might have been a fairer fight than Charles made it out to be. In fact, the brief glimpse of a limping child whose eyes grew in terror as she froze at the sight of them made Ethan wonder if this was less Charles's retaliation for an unprovoked attack and more his wish to finish what Alan had unfairly started.

Ethan searched for Liam in the half light of the moon but couldn't quite make out faces in the blur once the hunters started the attack. Suddenly the forest echoed with screams and howls from all around, and Ethan raised his crossbow out of instinct.

The thwack of an arrow just missing its target and embedding in a tree trunk distracted Ethan as he started to reach back into his quiver. Charles was three yards behind and to his left, screaming orders at him as he frantically pointed to a familiar figure darting away through the trees.

"Go, son! Go! Don't come back until you're wearing his flesh in victory!" Charles always knew how to phrase things, considering what Ethan had already done to that flesh.

Ethan ran after Liam, no plan in mind on how to avoid killing him, but it got them both away from Charles. He chased him for what felt like miles. His heart seemed close to bursting from the effort, and Liam was far more suited to running long distances than Ethan was.

Liam finally stopped running, and Ethan closed in on him, desperate to catch his breath. Liam didn't dare touch him or comfort him in case someone followed—from either side. Ethan knew Liam had heard the order Charles barked at him, and they both knew there were but two ways out of it unless they could think of a third and better option in a hurry.

Ethan felt Liam's eyes on him, and he met them with his own. Liam looked anxious, terrified for the first time ever.

Ethan bit his lip, desperate for a way out of this that ended with both of them alive. He clenched and relaxed his fists and shook out his fingers. "Run." There was no time to come up with a good plan, so a bad one would have to do.

Liam tilted his head. "What? This—you can't—"

"Run, Liam. Don't stop until you're safe. I'm the son of their leader. If I fall, they'll retreat for now. Get your people out of here as soon as you can. I don't know how long I can hold them off." Ethan formed the plan as he spoke. He would never be a great leader, but he would at least be alive in the morning.

Liam knitted his eyebrows together before understanding spread across his face. Ethan heard people coming. They didn't have long. He tossed his crossbow as far away from himself as he could and arranged himself on the forest floor as if he had been knocked out.

Liam defied Ethan's order long enough to kneel on top of him and kiss him violently, crushing his lips against Ethan's for as much time as he dared.

The last thing Ethan heard before Liam turned to run was a breathless, teary "Won't you ever learn that I care for you more than that psycho ever could?"

The plan worked as it should have. He feigned all the usual symptoms, playing them up as much as he thought he could get away with to distract Charles from blind rage, hoping there was some fatherly affection that still took precedence over his bullshit vendetta. Charles called for an immediate retreat, and there wasn't enough time for many injuries on either side. It was an odd definition of success, but Ethan would take it.

On the way home, Charles took turns berating himself and Ethan. Himself for rushing in without a better plan and Ethan for letting some "abomination" get the better of him.

Turned out it was Fi, with a long but mostly superficial gash across her back from a stray attack, who actually forced Charles to rethink things.

Still, they were safe.

He hoped.

He knew he wouldn't be seeing Liam for a while, and it hurt more than the knowledge that Liam was right about how little Charles cared for him. But worse than that was not knowing how long it would be until he had confirmation that Liam was safe.

Thankfully the news came the next day when he reluctantly cracked open his European History textbook to study and inside, slipped between the pages at the chapter's beginning, was a folded piece of paper.

He sucked in a breath and read.

OK.

No more information than that, but it was all he needed. Any more than that and Charles could have had major questions if he snooped around, and Ethan was suddenly very grateful for the simplicity of the note and of Liam's newfound discretion.

CHAPTER 7

WEEKS PASSED without incident. Without Liam. Charles locked himself in the garage for days, hammering and sawing, planning like a madman. Ethan avoided him as best as he could, but one afternoon Charles emerged and knocked on the door to his room.

"I need a drink, son. Some old hunting friends are passing through town tonight, and they want to have dinner, and I want my son with me."

It was not a request. Ethan sighed and wordlessly went to look for a nice shirt in his closet.

In hindsight, he should have known better, should have seen through Charles's bullshit, but he had been off his game for weeks and even if he didn't know the reason for it, Charles knew to strike when the iron was hot.

Ethan realized the "dinner with some old hunting friends" was actually the "set up my son and your daughter on a blind date for the perfect pair" five seconds in—five seconds too late to make an escape. Especially when Charles and the girl's father drove off to get drinks somewhere else.

The restaurant was one of the oldest in town, remarkable at that point for nothing beyond its forty-year-old sign boasting of having air-conditioning. In its heyday, it might have been a romantic spot, but romance was the last thing on Ethan's mind tonight.

Penelope was twenty-two and the daughter of a very powerful family from Georgia.

She was... tall. Good for her. She took her vitamins and ate her Wheaties.

She was blonde... with a bonus crispiness from so much hair spray that Ethan imagined it could double as sandpaper.

Her makeup was somewhere between clown and Great-great-aunt Sharon, who, at ninety-one, can't seem to find her lips as well as she used to.

Her voice was velvet... wrapped around gravel soaked in hydrochloric acid, and she talked of kills and calibers, and no twenty-two-year-old woman should sound like a seventy-eight-year-old man with a smoker's cough.

The more she talked, the more Ethan mentally checked out, and, hello, there was a hand on his thigh. She smiled coyly when he jumped and knocked the underside of the table painfully with his knee. He could only describe the look as terrifyingly possessive. And she had lipstick on her teeth. It complemented the spinach there well, though.

"Look, Ethan, I want to make this very easy on you." She ran her fingers up his leg. "No games, no wondering 'is she, isn't she.' Because she is. She totally is." She batted her eyelashes... or she had something in her eye. He couldn't tell.

"I have to go to the men's room!" He didn't care if that sounded as panicked as he felt when he stood, shrugging off the offending hand.

"Ooooooh, good idea. See if there's one of those condom vending machines in there, and we can skip right to 'dessert' when you get back." She waggled her eyebrows suggestively. Or suggestive of a stroke. Oh, God, he had to get out of there.

I'm walking home. Decision made. It might be storming outside, and the lightning would probably kill him, but he was willing to risk it and walk the fifteen miles home.

Penelope had a view of the front door, and also of his ass as he walked away from her, judging by the catcall she made. It sounded more like she was choking, but he got the general idea. And the general idea was to run out the back door before she suspected something.

He followed a server who had cigarettes in his hand to the back of the restaurant and out an unassuming single door where there was an awning and a picnic table. The server looked alarmed for a second, but Ethan held up his hands in a show of peace and walked out into the rain.

It was cold and windy, but he was not with Penelope, and that was all that mattered. In fact, Charles was going to be so pissed if he did make it home that death would be the preferable option all around.

He walked a few feet more, rounding the corner of the building, before his senses started to alert him to something. Or someone. Shit. It hadn't taken long for her to find him. She was a hunter, after all. He should have known better. He started to whirl around to explain himself somehow, but a dark, solid object was on him, flinging freezing cold water in his eyes and slamming him up against the rough brick exterior.

The cloaked figure held him against the wall with his weight and growled. Ethan struggled to free himself, but the figure held him tighter and finally removed the hood of his jacket.

"What's wrong? Weren't you having a good time with your future wife in there?"

Liam.

Ethan breathed again and relaxed against the wall. "What are you doing here?" *Where have you been?* But he didn't want to ruin this right then.

Liam grinned. "I got hungry."

Ethan was about to quip about the restaurant's semifamous lasagna when Liam leaned in and sucked on Ethan's neck, making it very clear just what he was hungry for.

"Liam, I'm sorry. I didn't know…. Charles—"

"Shhhhhh. It's okay. Do you need a ride home? I can get you out of here." Liam pushed away to look at Ethan.

Ethan bit his lip. Fifteen miles in a car in this rain would have put him home in less than twenty-five minutes, and Fi was home with one of her friends. There was no way she wouldn't notice he got home so quickly and without Charles. "Know of a place I can hide out for a while?"

"I know just the place." Liam reached out for his hand, and they ran together to Liam's car.

Liam turned over the engine and cranked up the heat when he saw Ethan shivering. It was a sweet gesture because it was only for Ethan's benefit; those damned wolf genes probably kept Liam toasty enough on their own. Ethan shrugged out of his jacket to find he was soaked through to his skin and removed his shirt as well.

Liam let out a choked little noise, one Ethan appreciated so much more than Penelope's wet honk of a catcall. He didn't move to throw the car in reverse with any kind of speed despite the desperate need to leave before Penelope came looking for him.

"Just seeing how much more you'll take off." He looked down toward Ethan's pants with greedy anticipation.

Ethan leaned close and felt the heat Liam was giving off and, in mock innocence, kissed him on the cheek before whispering, "Get me out of here, and I'll be naked before you hit forty-five."

Ethan had never seen a transmission fly out of a car before, but Liam slammed the gearshift so quickly it threatened to happen right then. Ethan kicked off his squishy shoes and socks and leaned his seat back so he could work on his trousers.

Liam glanced down every now and then to watch, and Ethan prayed those supernatural reflexes were working overtime as he drove through the storm.

He dragged his boxers down, and Liam swerved the tiniest bit. Ethan liked this show of vulnerability. Liked knowing he was responsible for it even more.

"You all right there, Liam?" he asked as he took his own cock in his hand and stroked a little.

"Jesus." Liam looked at the road ahead almost purposefully and let out a shaky breath. "Yeah, just fine, Ethan."

Ethan raised an eyebrow and smiled. "Really." He squeezed himself a bit so he would make a noise he knew Liam couldn't resist.

Liam adjusted himself in the driver's seat and shook his head. "Yep."

"Uh-huuuuh." Getting the upper hand on Liam was more fun than he ever expected. No wonder Liam spent so much time doing it to him. And speaking of…. "She touched me."

"What?" The growl that ran under the word should have terrified him.

"Yeah." He released himself and reached for Liam's right hand, nudging it off the steering wheel. "Right here." He placed Liam's hand where Penelope's had been.

Liam rubbed hard, possessive circles on the spot and slowly worked his way upward. "Did she touch you here?"

"Yeah."

He went a little higher. "Here?"

"Y-yeah." Liam's warm fingers on his cold skin were doing things to him. So much for the upper hand.

Liam ran a finger along the crease where Ethan's thigh met his hip. "Here? Tell me she didn't touch you here."

Ethan stopped breathing for a second, jerking his hips as Liam set the sensitive nerves there on fire.

Liam casually moved his hand to settle on Ethan's cock. "How about here?"

"Ooooh, God…. N-no."

"Good," he purred. "Wouldn't want to have to rip her… *pretty* little face off, would I?" He spread his fingers so he could wrap them around Ethan, but Ethan had other ideas right then.

He sat up a little and looked toward Liam in earnest. "Thanks for rescuing me, Liam. She was going to eat me alive. I know Charles wants me to marry into the business and all, but even if I wanted… she scares me."

Liam chuckled warmly at the thought of a hunter terrified of a girl. "You don't have to thank me, though. Just protecting what's mine."

Ethan licked his lips. "Yeah. Yeah, I think I do need to thank you." Before Liam could question it, Ethan leaned over and palmed the bulge in Liam's jeans.

"*Oh.*" Liam got it then. Ethan worked the button and zipper open, and Liam never took his eyes off the road as Ethan freed him from the slit in his boxers. "Oh, yeah. You can do that. You can totally thank me like that. I don't know what I was thinking before."

Then it was Ethan's turn to laugh as he leaned over the rest of the way and took Liam just barely into his mouth, licking around the head. Liam freed a hand from the wheel to stroke his hair, and Ethan thought it might be the best feeling in the world. He didn't feel the car swerve in any dangerous way, so he tested out taking him in a little deeper, sucking a bit, and it drew out a delicious noise and a tighter grip from Liam.

He settled into a nice rhythm, and it was not long before Liam started to squirm uncomfortably under him. "Ethan... God... Ethan, I gotta pull over. I'm gonna come. I don't know if...."

Ethan pulled off just long enough to order him to "keep driving." The rain had slowed, and there was no one on the long stretch of road that time of night. And maybe he believed in those reflexes more than he should.

Liam breathed in sharply, like he was going to protest.

"Keep driving, or I stop." And he pushed back onto Liam until he had taken him all in, speeding up the thrusts for emphasis. He was not fucking around. He was not thinking of Charles or Penelope or anything but Liam, and he wanted Liam to remember this and them like this for a long time.

Liam pressed on the gas pedal and accelerated into a turn. They must have been driving the back roads on the edge of town, but Ethan was not going to stop blowing Liam to find out.

"Oh, oh, fuck, Ethan. God, that feels so good."

Ethan tasted the bitter drops of precome beading up on Liam's cock, and he knew Liam didn't have long.

Liam kept his foot on the gas even as he lifted his hips a little. "Yeah, just like that. Mmmm...."

Ethan could only imagine the sight they would make if someone happened to drive by in a tall truck, and it just made him suck and thrust that much more obscenely. And the thrill of forcing Liam to focus on the road while he gave him so much pleasure made it even hotter.

He gave a few long sucks, hollowing his cheeks to make it as tight as possible, and Liam groaned and thrust upward once, coming fast and messy and loud, peppered with curses and moans, into Ethan's mouth. As he swallowed it down as best he could, much better this time around, Ethan noted with amusement that Liam did not swerve once.

Once Liam's cock stopped twitching, Ethan let him go and sat up, beaming at him with a certain pride, and Liam looked like a live wire ready to catch fire. Ethan wiped his mouth with the back of his hand and nodded as he made a show of rubbing the wetness on the exact spots where Penelope touched him earlier, putting that claim on himself for Liam.

Liam pulled into the next clearing and shifted into park. He flattened himself against the seat back and breathed for a few seconds, staring at the wet spot on Ethan's thigh.

"You okay?"

"That was so hot. God, Ethan. That was so hot." Liam turned off the car and unbuckled his seat belt. He didn't say anything else as he opened the car door and made his way to the backseat, pushing his jeans and boxers down and lifting his shirt up and off.

"What are you—?"

"Get back here." He didn't have to say it twice.

Ethan climbed into the backseat and into Liam's lap, into his warmth and his skin. Liam pulled him in for a kiss and reached for Ethan's neglected cock, softer now that he had spent so much time on Liam, but it was still very interested.

He stroked it slowly until Ethan was hard again. It didn't take long. Ethan moaned into his mouth more and louder as Liam sped up. He was not looking to tease Ethan tonight.

"Wanna see your mouth when you come. Wanna see the mouth that can make me come like that, okay? Can you still taste my come?"

"Yeah.... So good." He threw his head back so Liam could get a good view of him in the moonlight.

Ethan's hips ground down out of control on Liam, and it just made Liam stroke him that much faster until the pleasure overtook him and Ethan came in thick ropes that landed on Liam's chest and belly. He guessed he had marked Liam as well, left his own scent all over him, and that was how it should be.

Ethan collapsed into Liam, not caring about the wetness between them. They sat wrapped in each other until it finally did get uncomfortable and too hot.

It was still raining, and Liam got the crazy idea to wash off in the drizzle, after promising to run the heater on high until he got Ethan home. He felt like a savage, standing in the freezing rain, naked, but Liam couldn't stop kissing him, running his hands over him, and sucking off the water drops at his neck.

When he couldn't take any more of the cold, Liam reluctantly drove him toward home. Ethan turned the vents to face him and went quiet as an old Siouxsie and the Banshees song played low over the last of the rain and the hum of the engine.

Liam must have sensed the question Ethan didn't want to ask. "I didn't, you know. I hope you know that. I'd have been justified joining in, but *I'm not my father*."

Ethan sighed, knowing the emphasis served to remind him that he, too, was not his father, but *justified* floated before his eyes, a grim reminder that no matter how much they had in common, no matter how their morals lined up, they were still fighting on opposite sides. And a terrible confirmation as to who attacked first.

"I know, Liam. I know you wouldn't. But someday...."

Liam swallowed hard. "Someday I may have to, yes. Or someday you will. But not today, Ethan, okay?"

Fleeting images flew through his mind of fighting Liam on the battlefield, both ordered to by their demanding fathers. He shook his head clear and tried to put it out of his mind until much later.

Liam put a hand on Ethan's shoulder. "You gonna be in trouble?"

"Oh, yeah. Big time." He reached up to squeeze Liam's hand. "Worth it, though. You gonna sabotage all my dates like this?"

"Definitely. Especially if they touch you." Liam pulled behind a tree at the end of Ethan's street.

Ethan grinned as he kissed Liam good night. "Hmmm.... I should call Penelope and see what she's doing tomorrow, then." He laughed and opened the door, ducking one of his own shoes, which flew toward his head when Liam halfheartedly threw it at him.

He stepped out of the car and retrieved his shoe, hopping around to the driver's side. Liam rolled down the window so Ethan could lean in and pull him in for one last kiss. "Don't disappear for weeks like that again, okay?"

Liam smiled wryly. "I had to. To keep you safe. To keep *us* safe. I didn't want to, believe me. Besides, I think you're going to be the one to disappear for a while once Charles gets home."

Ethan didn't even want to begin imagining the punishment his father would relish doling out for his crime. He cringed, and Liam's face changed in an instant.

His voice dropped, low and dangerous; his smile was a distant memory. "If he hurts you…." Liam shrugged almost imperceptibly and tilted his head. "I'll kill him."

Something deep, primal, and biological told Ethan he should defend his father, but he couldn't bring himself to confront the statement. The rain chose that moment to start up again, signaling its intent with a loud clap of thunder.

"You better go, Ethan. We'll see each other again soon. No matter what the cost." *Ominous*, is what he should have been thinking, but he couldn't get past the idea of seeing Liam again. He was in so deep now. It was almost scary how things that had seemed so important once were becoming trivial now that Liam was in the picture.

The punishment was brutal, according to Charles. An old family secret that Charles seemed to have been waiting for years to spring on him, given the sadistic glee he displayed when he explained what Ethan would have to do.

The punishment for embarrassing the family name was banishment to the swamp for three days with nothing but a crossbow and seven arrows. It was survival in all forms. He had no shelter, no food, no water, and nothing but his skill to defend himself against any animal—or supernatural—he encountered.

It was so absurdly convenient that he almost grinned as Charles condescendingly laid out his fate.

Within ten minutes of Charles dropping off Ethan, who was trying very hard to look sullen and defeated, Liam came running into the clearing, having sensed him.

Liam could hardly keep a straight face as Ethan explained his situation.

"Wow. That's harsh. It sounds truly awful. Too bad you're not going to get to experience it and learn anything from it. You hungry?"

"I could eat, yeah." Three days in the forest sounded like heaven if Liam were there with him.

"Good. Let's get out of here. I'm so hungry I could eat a whole wild boar by myself." Liam started to walk away but turned back with a grin on his face. "But we're going to have burgers instead. Come on!" He laughed and pulled on Ethan's hand to get him to follow.

With no one looking for him, Liam decided a road trip was in order. "Where do you want to go? I'm thinking the beach, get a nice little motel room somewhere right on the water, and not get dressed again after I rip your clothes off with my teeth."

The thought was a distracting one, but he managed to decide on Cocoa Beach.

"My mom used to take me over there when I was little. Before she.... It was her favorite place in the world, I think. Charles would be out working or hunting, and he hated it over there anyway. She would wait until he left for the day and then drive me, and eventually Fiona too, to her favorite spot and we would sit all day and make sand castles and play in the tidal pools while we looked for little crabs and fish. She'd always end the day with an ice cream before driving us back. They are some of my best memories. I'd like to... I'd like to share that place with you, if you'll let me."

Liam didn't respond for a moment. He had a strange look on his face. "Ethan... I'd be honored."

"I'd also like to make some more good memories there with you, Liam."

Liam stopped in his tracks and kissed Ethan for a long time until the sound of a stomach growling dampened the mood a bit. Liam laughed. "Come on. Let's go," he said reluctantly.

It was difficult keeping their hands off each other on the drive over, but the anticipation of uninterrupted alone time and how they could spend it kept them from exhausting themselves too soon.

Ethan agreeing to be whisked away on a road trip over to Cocoa Beach had an unexpected benefit. There they could finally do something they hadn't been able to do before—go on a real date, in public, with no risk of being caught.

It took one drink to relax Ethan enough to think he could definitely get used to this, and three more to shake the sadness at the realization that there was little chance of that happening.

"What do you do when you're not rescuing me from crazy lady hunters and Charles?" It had suddenly occurred to Ethan around dessert that he knew nothing of Liam beyond what he saw when they were together.

Liam laughed. "What? What brought this up?"

Visions of Liam in a suit working in an office floated before his slightly buzzed eyes. "I mean, do you have a job? Do you spend your days chasing rabbits down by the lake? I really have no idea what happens when I'm not around."

Liam tilted his head and blinked a few times in mock offense. "…Chasing rabbits. You're going to pay for that one somehow, Ethan. And for your information, no, I don't have a job. I'm the eldest of five siblings, and it will be my job to take over when my father becomes too old to carry on anymore. I train. I learn. I even read. All my spare time goes to ensuring that I am prepared for that day. It will be my responsibility to protect my family from y—"

Liam cut himself off, but Ethan didn't have to hear the rest of it to know whom he was talking about.

Liam quickly turned it around. "Anyway, why do you go to school? Charles doesn't seem like the kind of guy who wants his only son going off to be an accountant or an engineer or whatever."

Ethan smiled wistfully. "Because I have to believe that this stupid war won't last forever."

Liam rolled his eyes. "A thousand years is pretty much forever, if you think about it."

"But, Liam, what if…." *What if we could end this war? What if we could be together and not have to hide it? What if we could really do this?* A million possibilities ran through his mind and he couldn't find a way to vocalize any of them.

Liam grabbed his hand and squeezed affectionately. "Yeah. What if, right?" He sounded sad but recovered quickly. "Besides, could you imagine me at a *job*? I'd be fired in a day no matter what I tried."

Ethan raised an eyebrow. "I'd hire you."

Liam smiled. "As what, may I ask?"

Ethan placed his free hand on top of the hand Liam still had on him. "Personal assistant. Clothing optional. Just be at my beck and call twenty-four hours a day, ready for whatever I need at the moment."

Liam's eyes narrowed at the absurdity of the notion. "You couldn't afford me."

"Who says I would pay you in money?" he shot back.

Ethan watched Liam's eyes go wide, and as good as he felt at that moment, there was a persistent undercurrent that these times were the calm before a mighty storm.

THEY FOUND a motel with a room right on the water and checked in for the night. Sure, the sheets were scratchy and the place smelled like old sunscreen and seawater, but they were together and alone and safe. There was no need to hurry and no need to hide, so they took their time on each other, exploring from head to toe with their hands, their lips, their tongues. Ethan learned where he liked to be licked and bitten and what he could do to make Liam's toes curl.

He relished teasing Liam by slowly kissing down his chest and stomach until he reached his cock in the most roundabout way possible. Liam whined, and it only made him go slower, licking long, wet stripes on the underside of it until Liam actually growled a little. When he finally felt like Liam had had enough, he parted his lips and took in Liam an inch at a time until his hips arched off the bed in frustration. Liam reached for Ethan's head gently, and that was just what Ethan wanted. He let Liam set the pace, and it was incredibly good to feel both out of control and safe. Ethan was so hard he couldn't wait any longer to take care of it, and he wanted Liam to focus completely on what Ethan was doing to him, so he used his free hand to stroke himself a little, to relieve some of the pressure building up in him.

Liam scooted up, taking Ethan with him, so he could rest against the headboard to get a better view. It wasn't long before Liam's cries got louder and more broken, and this time Ethan was ready. Liam came with a hoarse shout and Ethan swallowed him down, taking every drop as he listened to Liam's astonished and impressed breathy moans of "Oh my God" as Ethan kept him in his mouth through the last of the aftershocks.

He was still hard, so close to coming, and listening to Liam's contented sighs wasn't helping him calm down any, knowing he had made Liam feel that way. He stroked a little faster and harder and wished he had something to slick himself up with that didn't take much effort to get to, but Liam must have sensed his distress and pulled up on him. Liam was still leaning against the headboard and, on his knees and straddling him, Ethan's cock lined up perfectly with Liam's amazing mouth.

Liam's eyes went wide as he eyed Ethan's raging erection. He grabbed Ethan by the hips and licked his lips, surging forward fast and ruthlessly. Ethan looked down to watch his cock stretching Liam's lips as they turned red and spit-slicked, and the view was spectacular. Ethan came quickly. He grabbed the headboard for support and shuddered through an explosive orgasm that seemed to last for at least a minute.

Ethan collapsed on the bed, and Liam rested his head on Ethan's chest. They fell asleep soon after.

The morning sunshine peeked through the cheap drapes, and it took a minute for Ethan to realize where he was and who was with him. Once he came to his senses, he yawned and broke into a huge grin. Waking up next to Liam was amazing, and he was gorgeous even with his hair a mess from sleeping in the crook of Ethan's arm all night.

Liam stirred and pulled Ethan in for a kiss, and Ethan tried to protest on the grounds that he hadn't even brushed his teeth yet, but Liam ignored him and deepened the kiss anyway.

They managed to make it out of bed by 11:00 a.m., when Ethan's hunger became an uninvited guest in their bed.

Liam demanded pancakes for breakfast and Ethan laughed.

"Pancakes? The fierce wolf wants pancakes and not a rare steak or something? How am I supposed to feel about that?"

Liam shrugged, unperturbed. "Hey, you have your memories and traditions of childhood and I have mine. Saturday is always pancake day. Speaking of, after breakfast, take me to your spot on the beach. I want to see it."

They found a bustling breakfast place up US 1 that served really good pancakes, and when they'd had their fill, Ethan showed Liam where he'd spent those glorious, sun-soaked days before his mom died. He hadn't been back there since she had last taken him and Fiona, and it was bittersweet as the memories hit him.

Liam was patient and supportive as Ethan told of shark sightings and jellyfish stings and chasing seagulls that threatened to steal Fiona's lunch.

The beach butted up against a marine forest of old oaks and palmettos, and they decided to take a walk through it when the sun got too harsh. They eventually came upon a clearing studded with wildflowers and tall grass. They hadn't seen anyone else in the forest, so they rested there in the glade for a while, kissing and touching each other until they both became too aroused to get back to the motel before one of them would explode. They lay there hidden in the tall grass and stroked each other until they both came, and Ethan realized that, despite everything else going on, this was the first time he had truly been happy since before his mother died.

Ethan had to forgo shaving while they were there, a decision out of necessity to look the part of a man trapped in the forest for the weekend, but one Liam applauded when Ethan scratched his back with his stubble as he kissed his way down to the curve of Liam's ass on the second night.

They headed back to the forest on the morning of the third day and spent as much time getting dirty on the soft, wet ground as they could.

"For authenticity," Ethan rationalized.

"I don't care. You're going to smell like my forest." The hunger in Liam's eyes at the thought was an addictive look.

"I'm sure I smell like sweat and beer right now. Anything would be an improvement, I think."

But Liam was on him, pinning him against a tree and inhaling deeply at Ethan's neck, making him shiver when his hot breath rushed at him.

Liam inhaled again, this time licking a stripe of wet heat across his throat. "You smell like spice. Almost like cinnamon. And you taste like fire."

Ethan should have rolled his eyes and responded with a good-natured teasing for sounding like a cheesy romance novel, but Liam's mouth made its way to his, and anything he could have thought to say was gone.

When it was all over, Ethan was dirty, sweaty, covered in leaves and mud and scratches, and worn out enough to look the part of someone having roamed the swamp for three days straight.

Charles drove into the clearing just as Liam disappeared. If Charles was looking at his son with a smug grin, Ethan refused to look back at him and give him the satisfaction of noticing as they made the long drive home.

CHAPTER 8

"I THINK they're starting to suspect."

The late afternoon sun shined down into the small glade in the forest in which they had hidden themselves. Ethan had Liam's hand in his as they lay side by side on the grass and wildflowers.

"Who? Charles? Fiona?" Liam propped himself up on his elbows and looked at him inquisitively.

"Yeah, we're going to have to be careful—well, more careful. Maybe even stop seeing each other again for a while. If Charles catches us…. Liam, I can't even imagine what he'd do, and I don't want to find out. I would die before I let him hurt you, though." *I'd kill Charles before I let him hurt you,* is what actually ran through his head, but saying that out loud would have made those crazy, scary thoughts that much more likely to happen.

Liam looked stricken by the thought of once again not seeing him regularly. They both knew it was a possibility, the danger of getting caught. But they never really wanted to address it out loud. However, Ethan had to dodge Charles several times in the weeks after his secret trip with Liam. He had allowed him little to no personal space or privacy since he'd left Penelope waiting there at the restaurant.

Ethan heard Charles on the phone to Penelope's father not long after the incident. Ethan wondered if normal parents stuck up for their kids and lied when necessary, because Charles had no problem putting the fault squarely on Ethan no matter what Ethan had tried to tell him about Penelope's behavior.

Ethan was only there—back in Cocoa, their new sacred, hidden clearing they'd discovered together—because he'd convinced Charles he had an off-site lab for biology. That and he took the most circuitous route possible up through Daytona Beach, doubling back and back again until he was sure no one was following him.

"It's not forever, though. Just until things calm down. I promise." Ethan rolled over and laid his free hand on Liam's chest, encouraging him to lie back down.

Ethan had a surprise. He had been waiting for the right moment to spring it on him. Ethan reached into his bag and pulled out his camera.

Liam looked confused, but he smiled. "Seriously, Ethan?"

"Yeah. We'll get it developed here. No one in town will ever know. A copy for you and a copy for me. Just in case... you know. Now, lie back down."

Liam sighed but obeyed. "I guess asking you to run away with me is out of the question."

Ethan positioned his head next to Liam's and raised the camera so the lens looked down on them. "Yeah, because your people wouldn't hunt us down or anything. I'm sure they have some questions about where you go from time to time." He clicked the shutter open to take the picture. And one more for good measure. And maybe one more after that.

"Yes, and that's why I never let them near you. One slip and they'll know. They just think I go spying for information now and again and that's how they sense humans all over me."

"And do you?" He finally put the camera down.

"Do I what?"

"Spy."

"Yes. But for some reason, they don't care that you have the nicest ass I've ever seen or that I can make you come screaming my name that much faster if I—*oof*! Hey!"

Ethan threw himself on top of Liam and grabbed his wrists, pinning them up above his head, not caring that Liam could toss him off with a finger if he cared to.

"I was only kidding!" His face spread into a wide grin.

But Ethan had moved on. "What was it that makes me come screaming your name that much faster?" He lowered himself so he was inches from Liam's face, arching his head back a bit so Liam could scent his neck, something he knew drove Liam crazy.

Liam inhaled, and whatever he was getting off Ethan made Liam's hips jerk up. "Get naked and I'll show you."

Ethan happily obliged in a hurry. Liam joined him, taking a moment to visibly relax as the sunshine hit his skin. Ethan watched him, so free in his natural state, and wondered if Liam was the most beautiful thing he had ever seen—or would ever see—in his life.

"Is this it for a while?" Liam's eyes went wide as he stared at Ethan, like he was trying to remember every detail of him.

Ethan frowned and nodded. A few more weeks apart to take the heat off him, and maybe someday they would still stand a chance.

"Better make it good, then, I guess." Liam stretched out on the grass and invited Ethan to get back on top.

Liam must have known Ethan hadn't come empty-handed and retrieved his prize from Ethan's discarded jeans with minimal disruption. He set about slicking both of them up before he took their cocks together in one hand, sliding them together and thrusting his fist up and down, squeezing a bit for the most delicious friction. Liam knew him so well by then, knew the contrasting sensation of rough palm and smooth cock touching his own like that was foolproof.

Ethan felt himself go cross-eyed under Liam's touch. He was so hard it would have reduced a lesser man to tears. Liam was not going to let him come so quickly, though, despite his teasing promise.

Liam sat up, scooting them both so Ethan could straddle his lap. They kissed for a long time, Liam never letting go of their cocks. He reached up with his free hand to scratch at Ethan's chest, catching a nipple with his short fingernail, and it sent the sensation straight to Ethan's groin, making him hiss and arch his back.

As if sensing an opportunity, Liam nipped just slightly down Ethan's chest until he reached the hardened point. He lapped at it, laving the flat of his tongue over it until he saw fit to move on to the other one.

Meanwhile, Ethan was slowly going insane. He was noisy and breathless and was sure he had pierced Liam's skin trying to stop himself from going over the edge so soon.

"Want you, Ethan. Want to feel you on me, hear you call out my name, want your smell on me so I have something to get me through not seeing you for a while." Liam kissed him, messy and hard at the same time.

"Yeah, yeah, anything, Liam. Anything so when this is all over you'll come back to me." Ethan dived in for another kiss, but Liam stopped him short.

He looked hurt. "I will always come back to you, Ethan. Always. No matter what happens in the next few weeks or the next few decades, I will always come back to you. Why won't you learn? The war we're going to have to fight soon isn't going to change that."

Ethan opened his mouth to speak, but Liam shut him up with another kiss. "Don't. Not now, okay?"

Ethan nodded and wrapped his legs tighter around Liam, letting him take full control.

Liam pulled back to slick up his fingers some more. He pushed Ethan down flat and teased his legs open by kissing the insides of his thighs. Once he seemed satisfied with the view, Liam reached down to gently push his fingers inside, one by one, slowly, gently, letting Ethan get used to each one. It was not a sensation Ethan ever thought he would experience, much less enjoy, but Liam seemed to know just where to press in to distract him from the burn of stretched skin.

Ethan moaned and rode Liam's fingers as sparks of pleasure shot through him with every thrust. Ethan thought he couldn't possibly take any more of it, but Liam wasn't done yet. He wrapped his free hand back around his cock and pumped in rhythm with his fingers pushing in and pulling out.

"Ready to scream my name yet?" Like Liam didn't already know the answer.

"I don't want this to be over, Liam." But Ethan was so close.

"It's not forever." A slow smile spread across his face. "Still… it's not fair leaving you this way, is it?"

Ethan returned the grin. "Last time you said that, you kissed me."

"And did you think about it when I was gone?"

"I believe you saw me thinking about it. A few times." The blush no longer bloomed across his face when he thought of Liam watching him jerk off. In fact, the thought excited him.

Liam moved in closer so he could whisper in Ethan's ear. "Then I can't wait to see you think about *this*. I'm going to fuck you next time I see you, Ethan Robertson. I want to be inside you so badly it's driving me crazy. I'll get through this time away from you because I'm going to be imagining how amazing you're going to feel when you're tightened around my cock."

"Jesus…." Ethan's eyes rolled back in his head. Obsessing about their first time together wouldn't make their separation easier in Ethan's mind.

Liam smiled and slowly pulled out his fingers. He climbed on top of Ethan and took their cocks again. Liam didn't dare break eye contact or make a sound as he watched Ethan's every expression and listened to every hitched breath and whimper.

It was not long before Ethan came, as predicted, screaming Liam's name. Ethan wouldn't tease him, when he could breathe again, by pointing out that Liam came not much later, screaming Ethan's.

They held each other, naked, basking in the waning sunlight, until the sun fell behind the trees.

Ethan held on to the feeling, all the feelings, as long as he could into the night. He didn't sleep at all.

Despite everything, despite Liam and his father and the very real threat of war looming, Ethan still had classes. He refused to give up on the one normal aspect of his life, even if he did feel like death by morning.

It became normal in the Robertson household to see Ethan walking around like a zombie, and neither Charles nor Fiona thought twice to question him about it anymore. The pressure of trying to keep up with this ridiculous notion of school. Obviously.

He poured his coffee, ate his breakfast, and headed out the door with his books in tow, not noticing that the kitchen was strangely empty that morning.

He sleepwalked through his classes, relying on copying the annoying know-it-all Kevin Hughes—if he had to cheat, he at least had to have the wherewithal to cheat off the best student in school and buy him lunch every time he did—and his ridiculous mnemonic-riddled notes to at least keep him abreast in chemistry and calculus.

He felt like the undead when he finally walked back up the steps to his front door. Fiona was there to greet him, bouncing like a heroin addict on a sugar rush before he even got out his house key.

"Ethan! Oh my *God*! I'm so glad you're home! I have a surprise for you! Eeeeek! You're going to *love* it! And be *soooooooo* proud of your baby sister!" She ran behind him and jumped on his back, and she might have been all of one hundred pounds, but at that moment, she felt like a ton and he was already struggling just to keep himself up. He threw her off, but she remained unperturbed by his lack of excitement for whatever she was going on about.

"Jesus, Fi! You better have won the lottery or something because I'm fucking tire—"

"*Language*, Ethan! I'm a *lady*, and I deserve to be treated like one." She faked a pout.

"You, my dear, sweet baby sister, are a lot of things. But a *lady* is not one of them. Now what is this surprise?" He didn't have the time or the energy for much more of her drama.

She hopped up and down in excitement. "Okay, but I had to move it to the attic because it's taking up too much room downstairs! It's the greatest thing ever, and it's my first one *ever* and *aaaaahhhhhh*!" Her teenaged energy always got the best of her.

She led him to the attic. It was dark, lit only by the light at the bottom of the stairs. He could barely see as he ascended.

"Geez, Fi, can't you turn on a light or something? It can't be that great a surprise that I risk breaking my neck to see it." *What is she hiding up here?*

He reached the last step and she called out, "Okay, get ready!" Fi flipped on the bright light, and he shielded his eyes with his arm for a second to get used to it.

When he finally looked, he immediately wished he could never see again.

There, inside the cage his father had built for just such an occasion, half-naked, beaten to a bloody pulp, gagged, and bound by exposed live electrical wiring and thick silver chains, was Liam.

Ethan could vaguely hear the sound of his sister laughing at her own handiwork, begging for praise and taunting Liam at the same time.

He stared at Liam. Liam stared back. He was certainly awake now.

Fuck.

CHAPTER 9

"ISN'T HE *gorgeous*, Ethan? Red is definitely his color." The grin on her face was so like Charles it scared him. She turned to Liam, and Ethan could see light reflect off metal as Fiona slashed her field knife across Liam's face. Liam winced and fresh blood ran down his cheek.

"Fi, wha—" He breathed in, unable to finish.

The grin turned into a giggle, and maybe that quick change from sadistic hunter to praise-seeking child scared him more than anything else.

"Are you proud of me, Ethan? I got him all by myself. He was right here, Ethan. Right in our backyard, hiding in the bushes. I mean, who does that, right? A werewolf just happens to be lurking around a house full of hunters? Worst spy ever. Or worse, right? An omega." She spat out the word, throwing Liam a glance and daring him to react.

"Are you all alone, puppy? Got no pack to protect you?" She put on a mock sad face and ruffled Liam's hair. "Awww, poor puppy. Let's keep him, Ethan. I need the moving target practice."

Ethan gave Liam a quick once-over. Fiona's eyes glazed with the sadistic glee he had seen in Charles so many times in the past. He didn't seem to be missing any parts, but the bleeding and bruising was pretty bad and, of course, the voltage wasn't letting him heal. He spied a few holes in Liam's shirt, ringed by blood.

"Jesus, Fiona. How many times did you shoot him?" This was so beyond the realm of redemption. Fiona had to know how serious this was.

Fiona looked at her brother like he was an idiot. "Until he begged me to stop." She shrugged nonchalantly. "He was making such a good moving target too. Took eleven arrows just to bring him down. Then I ripped out a few and shot him some more just to be sure."

Like it was no big deal. Like she was unaffected by what she had done. Like all the warning signs of a senseless killer. Like Charles.

"And what was all this that came after?" He pointed to the bruises and cuts. "For information?"

She smiled and batted her eyelashes. "Ethan, I've already told you, I don't know if he's a spy or an omega. If I had tortured him for information, *I would have gotten information*. This?" She pinched the newest cut, making it bleed faster. "This was just for fun."

She blinked slowly, and the sadistic hunter was gone in an instant. She stood on her tiptoes and kissed her brother on the cheek.

"Anyway! I promised Daisy I would go mini-golfing with her today, so would you mind watching him until I get back? He won't give you any trouble, I promise! I'll be home before Dad gets home so I can show him myself!" She ran a hand down her shirt to wipe off the blood from Liam's cheek and looked down at herself. "Oh! I gotta get cleaned up and changed! Can't go out with blood all running down my shirt, silly me!" With a grin on her face, she bounced downstairs like she hadn't just spent hours torturing a man.

Ethan sat on a stool, frozen. He never took his eyes off Liam as they listened to the water running and footsteps and, finally, the front door slamming shut. With speed normally reserved for the supernatural, he shut off the electricity and untangled Liam from his myriad bonds, apologizing the whole time.

"Shit! Liam, God! I'm so…. Fuck, what did she do to you?" He found layer after layer of injury. Any normal human would not have survived it. He freed Liam's mouth, and Liam breathed in sharply, cringing through what must be a broken rib or five.

"I… underestimated your sister, it seems." With the last chain free, he slumped to the ground, and Ethan followed him to cushion him from the hard floor as best he could.

"What the hell were you doing here?" He could feel the ribs beneath Liam's skin starting to knit back together, and the cuts already looked a bit healed.

"Last night... I was coming to warn you. The pack has caught wind of your psychotic father's latest plans, and they're mounting quite a defense. I know you can't stop him, and I know I can't stop my pack, but, Ethan, protect yourself. For me. They're coming, and they're indiscriminate about who goes down in their wake." He was breathing better, but it was still ragged and wet.

"Can you walk?" He cradled Liam's head on his lap, watching the bruises fade as he carded his fingers through his hair to give him some pleasure with all the pain.

Liam smiled. "Keep doing that, and in a minute, I can fly."

"Good, because you're getting out of here, as fast as you can. How long till you're fully healed?" Ethan, out of necessity, had gotten better at improvising plans to save their skins.

Liam closed his eyes. "A few hours, maybe? I can't go home like this. They'll attack without warning, up their timetable. You'll have no defense."

"Can you get somewhere safe? There's a motel about a half hour out of town. On 33. The Sunrise. Can you get there?"

Liam reached up and touched Ethan' face. "Yeah. Yeah. Will you be there?"

"As soon as it's safe. Now, Liam. How's your hand?" This plan would not go down in history as one of his better ones.

Liam looked confused. "My hand?"

Ethan clenched his jaw. "Yeah."

"Fine?"

"Good. Punch me."

Liam sat up. "What?"

"How else did you escape? I'm unarmed. The electricity failed because it wasn't tested properly. You overpowered me and escaped. I came to later and went after you. Explains both our absences to Fiona and Charles. I'll see you safe and catch up with them later. Lead them astray. We'll deal with everything else later." Ethan stood up and prepared for the pain.

Liam followed, but he seemed rightfully hesitant.

"Liam, do it. It's the only way."

Liam bit his lip and breathed out, lost in thought.

"Liam. I'm ready. I can take it. Do it."

Ethan closed his eyes tightly and willed himself to relax. Instead of a sharp pain, he felt soft lips touch his own. Liam's face was wet with sweat and blood, but Ethan warmed to the taste of his skin quickly, copper and salt and *Liam*, kissing along stubble and avoiding the healing cuts as best as he could. Their tongues found their way to each other, and he melted into Liam despite the danger, despite running out of time, his sister, Charles, the war that was surely coming, and, mostly, he guessed, himself. He lost himself in the feeling of Liam's wet mouth. Sensitive nerves lighted like fire down his spine.

He barely felt the moment Liam's fist connected with his face until he was halfway to the floor.

CHAPTER 10

ETHAN OPENED his eyes slowly. It was a bit fuzzy. No, it was a *lot* fuzzy. But he felt the sting of a split lip and a swollen jaw, and that was all that mattered.

Still….

"Not one of your better ideas, Ethan." He thanked deities he didn't believe in that no one was around to see him because he didn't have to be stoic for himself.

He sat up in stages, touched the wound gingerly, and hissed. The pain wouldn't hold a candle to what he had to do next, though. A socked jaw was one thing. A socked jaw with unmistakable signs that Liam left him unable to follow was at least believable.

He sighed and wrapped a wrist with the electrical wire.

It was not juiced enough to shock him unconscious, but it hurt like hell and he could smell the beginnings of seared flesh. He gritted his teeth and watched as the tendons in his wrist tensed up, and when a mark appeared, he flipped off the current and repeated the procedure on the other wrist. A few well-placed shallow slices with a knife so his clothes were appropriately bloody and ripped, and he looked and definitely felt the part.

It had been twenty minutes at least since Liam left.

Ethan set about knocking things around to sell the lie of a struggle. He left a trail of blood on the floor mixed with Liam's, and he hurt everywhere, and the room was spinning, but he had to finish and get to Liam to make sure he was safe.

Satisfied with the mess, with the injuries and blood, he struggled down the stairs, lumbering with each step, angry that, as bad as he felt right then, Liam had had it ten times worse, and healing or not, he had withstood more pain than Ethan would ever be able to manage. He just wanted to get to Liam and take away any pain that remained, any memory of the torture his sister had inflicted on him.

And then he could deal with Fiona.

He drove, not caring that his car was getting bloody. He drove, numb but with purpose. Out of town, past the places his sister hung out, the urge to stop to find her, to break her until all she could do was scream, to make her feel a tiny bit of what Liam must have felt, rose so sharply he feared losing control.

Were he a less moral man, she would be hurting. Sister or not. Fifteen or not. Human or not.

The Sunrise Motel, set back in some old-growth pine trees, was appropriately rundown for a no-tell motel. Pay by the week or pay by the hour, and double check for spiders in the bathroom, but they kept the sheets clean, according to several of his high school friends who wanted a step up from car sex back in the day. And there was a decent diner and little store attached to it.

He pulled around back so no one could see him from the road, and he slowly emerged from the car, careful not to disturb his scabbing wrists. Before he could wonder how to find Liam, the door to room twenty-three opened and Liam was there in the doorway with ripped, dirty jeans on and nothing else. He saw Ethan and the blood and the knot on his face, and was on him in the span of two breaths.

Ethan felt his warmth and scanned quickly for any unhealed injuries before he collapsed into Liam's grip.

"Ethan, what the hell did you do?" Liam adjusted his hold to avoid Ethan's wounds and helped him into the room.

It smelled like damp and a halfhearted attempt at disinfection from the so-called housekeeping staff, and it was dark with the drapes drawn. Liam sat him on the bed and started pawing at him, learning every cut and bruise before disappearing into the bathroom for soap, a cup of warm water, and a scratchy, threadbare washcloth.

"Why, Ethan?" He got on his knees in front of him and set about tenderly undressing and cleaning every slice and every burn, but even the gentlest touch was like fire on Ethan's flayed skin.

"Because no one would believe I just let you go without a fight. The chance of a wolf coming back for revenge on Fiona would be the only thing on their minds, so I would be breaking the rules by letting you go. And you're technically her catch. I should merely respect her wishes, whether she is following our rules or not." He struggled to get the words out as Liam continued to clean his tender, broken skin.

Liam rolled his eyes. "Ah, yes. A convenient weapon for hunters. And how does catching me and torturing me for hours play into the laws of hunting, Ethan?"

"Fiona will be punished accordingly, but—"

"But not with the same intensity she punished me, right?"

Ethan supposed it was a fair question, but he also got the underlying meaning of it. He closed his eyes. "No. It doesn't work that way. Humans, human children, especially, even ones who...." He reached out for Liam, to touch his face, his hands, anything in his reach.

Liam leaned into his touch, but it was an uneasy gesture. "I'd call it unfair, but you and I both know that your sister will be marked if my pack finds out she takes and tortures wolves who pose no immediate threat. I can't stop that. It's our 'rule,' child or not. And they won't stop until either she's dead or they are... and judging from what I saw today from her, I honestly don't know who'd come out on top in that fight. Ethan, I may have been her first, but she won't hesitate to do this again to more of my kind. She and Charles are starting a war that they can't finish alone. And they're going to drag you down in it."

Liam cupped Ethan's jaw and guided him closer. "But we're safe now. All of us. Right now. Ethan, I can't guarantee when I will see you again after tonight. It's too dangerous. For my pack and your family both. I can't stop my pack from retaliating against your father and Fiona, and your family is too insane to listen to reason."

It had come to this—a war neither he nor Liam wanted to fight, and yet they would be forced to pick up their weapons and draw lines in the sand.

"I want to protect my pack, and you want to protect your family. No force in the world can stop that. And when it comes to that moment, we'll have to choose our sides." His lips brushed against Ethan's, and he flicked out his tongue to taste the salt on his lips.

"So what do we do until then?" Ethan palmed the sides of Liam's neck and brought him in for a full kiss.

"We lay down our armor." Liam, still careful of Ethan's wounds, surged forward and pushed him down on the bed, crawling on top of him until they lined up perfectly. They kissed for a long time, and Ethan was desperate to hide the tears behind tightly shut eyelids.

Liam wiped away the wetness on Ethan's cheeks and forehead and kissed him almost sweetly on the forehead.

"It's now or never, Ethan. I don't know how this will end. I don't know if we'll ever have the chance again. You're going to grow up, get married, have hundreds of babies, and I'm going to be the head of my own pack someday, and we're going to fight and forget, and I can't, I don't want to, not any of that without having this one night with you. Please. Give me this before we have to go."

Ethan opened his eyes, and all he could see was blue, blue, blue, and Liam murmured under his breath that he would never see anything, anyone else, even when he dreamed at night, and Ethan opened his eyes wide and swallowed thickly.

He nodded slowly and bit his lip. "Yeah, okay, yeah."

And it was all the approval Liam needed.

Liam pulled away and stood to shed his bloody jeans, the last bitter reminder that it was Fiona who was at the heart of their undoing. Ethan lifted his hips to shove down his boxers, and then it was nothing but warmth and comforting weight on top of him, Liam kissing him deeply and with a need that burned through him. Ethan grabbed at skin, at anything he could get, as the kisses reached a frenzied pace.

He should have been in too much pain to get hard, but he responded to the desperate touches and tiny moans that escaped Liam's lips. He pushed his hips against Liam, arching his back, and Liam sighed against his mouth like it was all he ever wanted.

Liam pushed his hips away and hovered over him on all fours. He bent down and found a nipple and licked at it, causing Ethan to cry out. He gave equal attention to the other one and took it a step further by nicking it ever so slightly. He lapped at the drop of blood that seeped out, and Ethan watched with fascination, chest heaving. Liam ran his fingers across Ethan's ribs and pushed so he would turn over. Ethan rested his head on his arms and let Liam's fingers explore his back and work their way lower.

The moment he heard the click of a tiny bottle cap—lotion or something, he guessed—everything else seemed to melt away. The very real danger they were in, the consequences of their actions, the crushing fear that this might be the only time they would ever make love, and the almost crippling sadness of knowing that what they did now would forever lie in the shadows and ruins of whatever happened afterward. All those emotions and damning thoughts should have overshadowed the magnitude of this moment, but with Liam here, he could easily push that away until he only felt safe and wanted.

He spread for Liam without hesitation, and Liam softened the moment by kissing down his spine as he slowly, torturously entered with one finger. Ethan rutted against the bedsheets, fisting them in tight bunches while Liam thrust in and out until the burning stretch subsided and—no rest for the weary—he added a second, just as slowly and just as tenderly. Ethan couldn't stop the stream of nonsense from flowing— a litany of "yes" and "fuck" and "Liam" rolled into one long moan.

"So good, Ethan. Almost ready to be inside you." Liam sped up his thrusts a bit, moving his fingers apart slightly. "Ethan, I can't... it's going to hurt. I can do this all night, and it's still going to hurt."

"Do it, Liam. God, please!" *Now or never.* The words ran through his head over and over in rhythm with Liam's fingers slowly threatening to drive him out of his mind. *Now or never.* He had stayed so strong, so vigilant since he'd met Liam. He could not be expected to stay patient as well. *Now or never.* It was the idea of "never" that terrified him.

Liam slid his fingers out and Ethan shuddered at the feeling. He listened to his own heartbeat drumming insanely in his chest as Liam slicked himself up as best he could with cheap hotel lotion. He poured some more on his fingers and did the same for Ethan, determined to make it as easy as possible.

Liam hovered inches from him, and his breath hitched. Ethan knew this was it. He felt Liam descend on top of him. The head of his cock pressed against him, slick and demanding, and, fuck, yeah, it hurt as Liam pushed in slowly and gently, and he wanted to pull away, but Liam held him down and planted kisses on his shoulders, and the pain soon ebbed away, leaving an incredible closeness, a fullness, a feeling of being part of someone in a way he hadn't managed before in three years of college sex.

Liam hadn't breathed out yet, hadn't moved, as if he were waiting for an okay to keep going, and he got it with the breathy "Liam, yes" from Ethan.

And then it was nothing but the glorious harmony of two people sharing in each other's pleasure, thrusting and moaning, whispering names and breathing in little hitched, choked-off breaths.

Liam yanked them both up to their knees, pushing both of them closer to the headboard so Ethan wouldn't have to bend his wrists too far for support. Ethan took the opportunity to reach down and grasp his own erection and used Liam's thrusts to push into his fist.

"Oh, God, yes, Ethan. Going to feel so good when you come."

Ethan stroked faster, feeling the tingle rush down from his head to his dick. Liam's fingers dug into his hips, holding him in place, and the threat of claw on the sensitive skin there ripped the orgasm from him. With a shout he spilled over his hand and on the bedsheets and headboard. He was not yet steady, even on his knees, but Liam wrapped his arms around Ethan's chest and continued to thrust through Ethan's orgasm and the aftershocks.

"So, so good. Just like I thought." Liam snaked his arms around his shoulders and pulled, and then they were both just on their knees. Liam held him upright, letting his head rest so he could kiss Ethan on the neck, nipping and sucking at the marks he made there.

"So close." Liam barely whispered. "So close, Ethan. I don't want it to end."

But it did. It had to.

Liam's orgasm was bittersweet. He held Ethan close throughout it, repeating his name over and over as he came.

They both collapsed on the bed, breathless, and lay there for a long time.

When Ethan dared to look at the clock, he realized their time was up. Fi would be home, missing her capture and her brother, finding the signs of the struggle and the blood. She would be rushing to get Charles, and Ethan needed to wander in soon, beat up and breathless like he had been searching, and lead them on a wild goose chase, promising Liam went "that way, I swear."

Only his desire to keep the upcoming war from starting that night got him up off the bed and dressed. His desire for Liam that slowed him down, fighting every moment, every button to button, with a kiss, a touch.

Charles would set his psychotic plan in motion even without the specific target who escaped his daughter and his son, and Liam's pack would surely retaliate, because that was how the worst wars started.

"Where will you go?" Ethan was down to his last article of clothing to put back on—his shoes. He laced the first one with more time and care than it needed.

"North. For now. I won't go back to my pack until I am healed fully. But I'll still have to answer for my injuries. They'll sense it even if they can't see them anymore. The smell, you see. It won't go away as quickly, and my absence will raise questions. Fiona's still technically a child. They might be lenient, but she'll have to answer for it. I'll reason with them to be rational. For you. But do not mistake my feelings for you as forgiveness for her. She committed a crime against us, by your own admission and your laws too. And she'll do it again. I won't lie to my pack about the circumstances behind my injuries." Liam spoke with such authority, if he were talking about anyone else but Fiona, Ethan would be proud.

But Liam was indeed talking about his baby sister. "Then I guess the lines are drawn." It was not a threat. Ethan leaned in, and they met for one final kiss. It was brutal and messy, and there was an unspoken good-bye in it, each knowing this was it. They broke apart, and Liam took Ethan's hand as they left the motel room together.

He walked Ethan to his car, Ethan's fingers wrapped tightly around Liam's because he was not ready to let go. Ethan reached for his keys with his free hand but stopped when he heard the too-familiar sound of a shotgun cock.

"Oh, big brother. Tell me this isn't who you've been secretly fucking all this time? Is it? You've been fucking a werewolf? A

Kinnaird? A Kinnaird I caught and then you, what, let him go, made it look like he escaped so you could go back to fucking him?"

Fiona.

She shoved Liam aside with the barrel of the gun and seized Ethan's left wrist. She sucked in a breath through her teeth when he winced. "Oooh, that looks like it hurts, Ethan. Did you actually give yourself electrical burns for my sake? Why in the hell would you go through all that for him? Do you... oh, fuck me, I can't even." She rolled her eyes. "Do you *love him?*"

Liam growled behind him. It was low and would scare the living hell out of any normal person, but Fiona just laughed. "Down, boy."

Ethan put himself between Fiona and Liam. "Fiona. Stay out of this. How the hell did you even find me?"

Fiona's eyes crossed for a split second like she couldn't believe the stupidity surrounding her. "You fucking moron. You think I really thought it was a coincidence there was a werewolf lurking around? You've been all moony for weeks, and I saw the look in his eyes when I mentioned you were on the way home so I could show you. I saw the way you looked at him when you saw him all tied up and hurt. It's not hard to put two and two together when you're dealing with *fucking idiots.* So, tell me, brother, *do you love him?*"

Ethan looked at Liam. He opened his mouth to speak.

"Whoops! Time's up, Ethan! You may love him. You may want to run away and be his mate forever and ever and adopt little babies and live happily ever after, or you may hate him so much you'll celebrate his death, but he'll die no matter what."

She raised the shotgun and took aim.

CHAPTER 11

"FIONA, *NO!*" Ethan threw himself between the barrel of the shotgun and Liam, shielding him and preventing his sister from covering up a stupid mistake by making a bigger one.

Fiona snorted in derision but did not lower the gun. "You'd sacrifice yourself? *For him?* A wolf, Ethan? Jesus Christ, I might use this on myself when I'm done with him. Save my future children from the shame of having an uncle who fucks werewolves." She rolled her eyes again, but refocused in an instant. "Get out of my way, Ethan. Let me finish this. He's my catch and mine to do with as I please."

Ethan didn't move save to grab Liam's hand. "No, Fiona. He's mine. And you will leave him be. He is not a mindless monster. You have no proof he has killed or will kill, and *you are breaking our goddamned laws.* Now drop your weapon and make this right."

"Oh, yeah, right. So he can retaliate and kill me? You're choosing him over backing me up here? Look at you. Look at how even now you can't keep your hands off him, even if it means dying with him. And I thought *I* was fucked up. Dream on, Ethan. *And step aside.*"

Ethan said nothing, but trained his glare on his sister and refused to look away.

"Fine, have it your way. I'll kill him anyway. The silver in here will leave just enough of a corpse. I'll drag his body back to Dad, and won't I just be that much more in his favor when I tell him that, not only did I bag it myself, but it's also the carcass of your abomination of a lover. How do you think Dad will feel knowing his only son is a wolf-fucker, hmmm? No matter what you say in your defense, he won't believe you. He'll believe *me*."

"Fiona, no! This isn't the way! You fucked up. You can make it right. Let him go, and I'll take you away, far away. I'll take you from this mess of a life Charles raised us in, and you can have a chance at a normal life!"

Fiona smiled and shook her head, so much older in this moment, and he knew then she was well and truly lost to the cause.

"It's too late, Ethan. I can't go back now. And I don't want to. I'll take him down, and I'll take his whole pack down too." Her finger was on the trigger, and he knew better than to underestimate her aim. She could hit Liam with pinpoint accuracy, just like a Robertson should.

And the world moved in slow motion.

Ethan threw an arm behind him and took Liam down with him as he ducked, like Liam didn't possess the faster reflexes, but it was instinct, the sharp need to protect him. The loud crack of the bullet leaving the barrel disoriented Ethan for a split second, and he felt pressure on his head he didn't understand until he saw Liam leap over him, fangs glinting in the fading sunlight.

And Liam was on top of his sister. He knocked the gun out of her reach, and she screamed, begging Ethan for help as she lay on the concrete.

Liam held her down and howled. "Not so tough now, are you, bitch?"

She struggled against Liam, and Ethan watched helplessly for a moment as they fought. He was going to turn her, kill her, tear her apart. The wolf had taken over, and it was all revenge and justice for the hours of pain she had caused him. And it was protection for his pack too, and any other pack she might encounter, because—Liam's feelings for him aside—Ethan was not their kind, and a pack will always make the choice to protect their own. And now Ethan had to make that choice too.

"Ethan, please! Help! Please!" The terror in Fiona's eyes snapped him out of his daze.

Liam's teeth were a hairsbreadth away from sinking into Fiona's skin when Ethan yanked him up with a strength he shouldn't have had. Liam yelped, and Fiona rolled away, toward the shotgun.

"You will not hurt my sister, Liam." He had Liam by the scruff of the neck, and Liam's eyes glowed, staring him down.

"I deserve justice for this. She came after *me*. I am owed this honor." He was breathing heavily, growling with each exhale. "I won't let her do this to anyone else."

"Then you'll have to kill me first, Liam. Or kill me in her place, but she is a child and I will take responsibility for her actions. *I won't let you harm her*." Fiona stepped forward to stand alongside her brother with newfound confidence at his courage. She nudged the shotgun into his hands and let him take control of the situation.

Liam blinked slowly, and Ethan could see the realization hit him.

"Then I guess this truly is good-bye." Liam's fangs were fully extended. His arms hung down at his sides, but Ethan could see his claws were out.

Liam breathed out one last breath. "I love you, Ethan."

Ethan raised the shotgun. "I love you too, Liam."

CHAPTER 12

ETHAN, BLINKING back tears, cocked the shotgun, but Liam was not looking at him anymore. Something in the distance behind Ethan made him go pale, and if he were anyone else, it would be a distraction, a ruse to buy some time, but with all his senses sharpened, above the din of his own heartbeat, he heard the snapping of twigs and the shuffle of pine needles. Liam rolled his eyes, and it was as much quiet panic as Liam could possibly muster, but Ethan wouldn't turn around. He hoped Fiona was backing his play, because this was her fault and stepping up was the least he could demand from her.

A slow clap sounded in his ear, and it wasn't from Fiona.

"Well, well, son. Looks like we have a situation here, don't we?"

Ethan breathed out and closed his eyes. His brow furrowed in resignation and dismay.

Charles.

Ethan blinked slowly as Charles handed his daughter a length of chain and walked with purpose toward Ethan. He sidled alongside the shotgun, still aimed at Liam, and raised his own weapon.

"And just tell me, boy. How long have you been fornicating with this *abomination*? How long? Weeks? Months? Long enough to think you love *him*? All those times I trusted you when you said you were going shooting or to the library you were, what? Sneaking off with him. Oh, but that wasn't enough, was it? Not for love. How many times has this thing been in my house, under my roof? How many times did you risk your life, your little sister's life? How many times have you disrespected this family? How many times did you disrespect *me* allowing this *thing* into my house?"

Ethan didn't speak. He didn't look at his father.

Charles leaned in close. He whispered, knowing Liam could hear every word. "Oh, I'm going to enjoy this. You don't get to destroy everything we stand for, you little bastard. You're not going to kill your lover. I won't give you the pleasure of seeing him die quickly. I'm going to kill him myself. And you're going to watch everything I do to him to make him suffer before he dies. There won't be a body to mourn when I'm done."

Ethan sensed Liam stiffen, and they both knew that between Fiona and Charles, any move he made would be met with a silver bullet that wouldn't miss its mark.

Charles pushed Ethan's shotgun down and walked up to Liam. Fiona followed with the chain and began to tie him up.

"You think you can fuck my son and get away with it? I knew you animals weren't as smart as humans, but I didn't think you were completely stupid, screwing the son of a hunter. My son may be confused and naive and think he's in love, but you, you don't get the same *consideration* I will give my human son. I'll enjoy every second making you die as slowly as possible. I'll take you apart and savor every scream, every plea to just kill you already, every strip of flesh I peel from your body. But not half as much as I'll enjoy using you to teach my son a very valuable lesson."

And yet, Liam was smiling.

Fiona chained him up well, and Charles drew back a fist and punched him square in the face. Liam recoiled but recovered quickly, still smiling.

"You think love will save you, monster?" Charles punched him again.

"No. But they will."

Charles had the courtesy to look confused for the split second before figures leaped out of the darkness and grabbed him and Fiona.

Ethan tried to raise the shotgun again, but he was taken from behind. Charles's advantage was gone. They were hopelessly outnumbered. Fiona struggled against her captor, and Charles was bleeding pretty badly. More dark figures emerged, and one of them freed Liam.

Liam rubbed his wrists and motioned to the pack. There were growls and wordless conversations, and Ethan didn't understand any of it. If he were honest with himself, he didn't care if he died tonight, because living meant no Liam and a hell of an impossible mess to clean up with his family.

Fiona was crying. Ethan watched her in the grip of a wolf, held tightly by claw and supernatural strength. He might not have cared about himself, but he didn't want his sister to die, no matter how sick she really was.

"Fi. Fi, calm down. I'm going to get you out of here."

The problem, though, was that he didn't know how. Fiona looked up at her brother. Her eyes were wet, and her face was dirty from the mud caked on the creature holding her. She was shaking and couldn't stand up straight in his grasp.

"I'm sorry, Ethan. I'm so, so sorry. I never meant…. I never. Ethan, we're going to die right now, and it's all my fault. I just wanted to protect you from making a big mistake, and I thought I could. Ethan! Please forgive me! Please forgive me before I die!"

Fiona started to choke. The wolf had tightened his grip on her throat, and she was panicking. Ethan tore at the wolf holding him, determined to save her before he died. He was not strong enough, though, and he heard a barking laughter echo through the pack.

Liam howled, and whatever it meant, the wolves loosened their grips on Ethan and Fiona ever so slightly.

He approached Ethan, eyes burning, teeth bared, and it was terrifying.

"It ends here. Everything ends tonight. I have a duty to protect my pack, my family. Take your sister away and never let us see her hunt again. She is still young. She has you to guide her. She can still change. Because if she ever hunts again, you will both die, and I won't stop it from happening. Don't make me live through that, Ethan. This is her only chance. I love you, Ethan. But I *will* kill you."

Ethan nodded and felt the wolf holding him release him when Liam signaled to him.

Ethan should have run, should have fought the wolves holding his sister and his father. It couldn't end like this. Despite Charles and Fi and an entire pack of wolves straddling a very thin line between murder and escape, he leaned forward and kissed Liam.

He didn't care. He couldn't care. It couldn't end in fire. He couldn't let Liam go with anger and resentment. Liam growled but responded to the kiss, hands weaving up to Ethan's face, his neck, gripping tightly because they were going to have to part soon—as enemies.

"I love you. I love you. I love you." Ethan whispered it over and over against Liam's lips until Liam pushed him away, wiping tears away with the back of his hand.

Liam smiled, and it was bittersweet, sad. He cupped Ethan's jaw. "Always," he whispered.

Ethan watched as Liam turned away. He caught his first real glimpse of the wolf inside him, all fangs and claws and quiet rage. Liam growled, an unnatural, primal sound that was sadness and defeat and victory and vengeance all together. The pack joined in with wild, frantic yips that grew louder as he approached Charles.

One glance back to Ethan, and there was a look on Liam's face he had never seen before.

"But we can't let this go completely unpunished. This is not Fiona's fault. Not completely. She was only following orders, right?"

Before Ethan realized what was happening, Liam raised his hand. The moonlight reflected off his claws a split second before they found their way to Charles's neck, slicing into it with a quick, neat swipe.

Fiona screamed, and Ethan lunged forward, but he was caught by strong hands.

There was resignation and guilt in Liam's eyes when he looked from Charles's quickly dying form back to Ethan.

"You're giving the orders now, Ethan. Don't fuck it up like your father did." With a howl, Liam and his pack leaped back into the forest and were gone.

Ethan froze in shock for several moments as Fiona ran and collapsed at their father's body.

CHAPTER 13

THEY DIDN'T go home until the next night. There were cops and paperwork and questions and lies, and Ethan didn't remember there being this much red tape when their mother died.

He needed to make decisions. For him and for Fiona. At twenty, he was physically and legally capable of taking on the responsibility to finish raising her, but the damage between them was done, and he didn't know if either of them would ever want to heal the rift.

For now, for the summer at least, she could stay with their grandparents in Boca Raton. It was the only decision he felt comfortable making that night.

He could hear the shower running and slipped into her room to throw a few things in her bags—clothing and a few personal effects. He placed them on her bed, a passive-aggressive gesture to let her know there was no point arguing with him. Their grandparents would be here within the hour. They would stay through the funeral and leave with Fiona that evening.

A half hour later, Fiona walked into his bedroom. Gone was the sadistic daughter of Charles Robertson, the skilled hunter with the deadly aim, his once giggly fifteen-year-old baby sister. He looked at her and saw nothing but a devastated, scared little girl. Fiona was a mess. He was torn between hatred and pity for his sister, and they still hadn't really talked about things—not that he wanted to.

He didn't know how to feel. With Charles gone, he was free. With Charles gone, he was orphaned. With Charles gone, he was left to pick up the pieces. And he couldn't forget that, at the end of the day, the man he loved had killed his father, no matter how bad his father really was.

"Ethan, I'm...." She sighed, as if not knowing how to finish.

Ethan looked away, swallowing down the infinite sea of loss and sadness that threatened to drown him. "Fiona, just... leave."

She blinked a few times, on the verge of tears, but she licked her lips and nodded. "Okay." She retreated to her room to finish packing.

It was the last conversation the Robertson children would share for a very long time.

AFTER THE funeral, Ethan wished he was feeling something other than *relief.*

With their de facto leader dead, the hunters who didn't scatter immediately to look for other more organized and successful family groups to join turned to Ethan for guidance, and he had none. He wanted to run, take Fiona far away, and start over in a place that knew nothing of the supernatural mess they had here.

The hunters wanted Ethan to demand vengeance, and he couldn't bring himself to retaliate.

"It ends here." He echoed Liam's words. "My father is dead because of this war, and it's gone on so long no one can remember why we are fighting in the first place." He was just so *tired.*

Almost no one agreed with him, but he didn't care. He was out now. He had hung up his weapons and, as the last male Robertson in this part of the family line, ended their involvement in the fight.

Weeks passed. He got up, went to school, and went home. Sometimes he slept in his car at night, parked in the forest. He felt closer to Liam this way, with the windows down to let in the fresh night air. He would fall asleep watching the moonlight dance through the trees and on his skin. He would fall asleep to the distant howls of wolves.

After one such night, he awoke to find a note on his windshield. On it was nothing more than an address and a time, but Ethan knew who it came from.

He debated whether or not to go, to meet again with the man who had killed his father, the man he desperately loved, the man who could break his resolve with a look.

In the end he went. He would always go, and Liam must have known that. The address was a rundown old citrus packing plant on the edge of the city. Neutral ground.

It was dark, but in the low light of the streetlamps shining through the broken windows, he could see Liam leaning against a pillar in the center of the room. He tried to be strong, to not break as soon as he made eye contact, but everything that had happened since that night overwhelmed him all at once, and he fell into Liam's arms like nothing bad had ever happened between them.

Liam held him tightly, sighed against him like, for one moment, everything was right again, but in an instant, he changed, stiffened against Ethan.

Ethan pulled back. "What? What is it?"

Liam ran his hand down Ethan's cheek. "I—I'm leaving. Tonight. Forever."

Ethan started to protest, but Liam went on.

"Ethan, it's the only way. I wish it weren't, but—"

"No, Liam, please!" Ethan broke down and hung his head.

Liam leaned in and kissed him softly at first, but Ethan deepened the kiss until it was messy and desperate, and only when they couldn't breathe anymore did Liam pull back and rest his forehead on Ethan's.

"There's no other way."

"Where are you going?" Ethan pushed back tears.

Liam smiled and carded his fingers through Ethan's hair. "I can't.... They've—" He sighed. "Part of the condition of my punishment is that we never speak again. You can't come find me, and I can never come back. Killing Charles, Ethan, I'm not proud of that, but killing him saved my life. And yours too. They were going to kill all of your family and me if I hadn't. You first, so I would have to watch every moment of your death. I couldn't bear that thought.

"It lessened my punishment, but I still must carry out what is left of it. I would rather go my entire life never seeing you again than knowing you are dead because of me.

"I never expected to fall for a human—for you. A hunter, no less. But I wouldn't trade that time with you for anything."

He kissed Ethan again, this time slower and deeper. It felt like good-bye to Ethan, and there was no stopping the flood of tears now.

"What happens if you disobey your pack?" There had to be a way out.

"They kill you. It won't be quick either. And they will force me to watch. Don't make me ever watch you die, Ethan."

"But what if I—I'm not fighting anymore. What if everyone else—" Ethan wildly recalled their conversation over dessert in Cocoa Beach. *What if....*

"If we end this war for good?" Liam smiled. "The moment that happens, I will come running to you."

"But what if we never have that second chance? Liam, I can't live without you!" Ethan couldn't believe they were saying good-bye again.

"And I can't watch you die! But believe me, Ethan, I will spend the rest of my life looking for a way to be with you again. We found each other once. We can do it again. I refuse to say that this is the end."

Liam wouldn't stop touching him. The haunted look on Liam's face told Ethan all he needed to know about what had gone on in Liam's pack after they had parted last.

Ethan slumped down, defeated. There really was no other way. He rubbed his hands on his face in a last-ditch effort to regain his composure before he spoke. "Okay. Okay, Liam." His resolve was steel. He was strong enough to do this. He knew it was the best thing for everyone.

He was also lying to himself.

"Go now." *Before I break. Before I take you away and damn the consequences. Before I convince myself it's better to be dead than live without you. Before I can say no to you.*

Liam's lips formed a tight line as he nodded his head in agreement. "Okay." He sighed and looked away, but turned back quickly and smiled, a gesture both sad and heartbroken. "But first...."

They made love: slow, bittersweet, through tears and the devastating good-byes. They made love face to face, savoring each touch, each kiss, each whispered "I love you" until they could delay the inevitable no longer.

Ethan dressed slowly and never took his eyes off Liam. Like if he did, he would disappear before one last good-bye.

"Do you still have our picture? The one from Cocoa Beach?" Now Ethan's most prized and hidden possession.

Liam smiled. "Yeah. I do. I'm taking it with me. Can't let go of that, can I?"

"Good. Good. I hid my copy in an album behind a picture of some of my old friends at the beach last summer." It was small talk meant to prolong this, but it wouldn't work forever.

Liam pressed his forehead against Ethan's. "Look at it. A lot. Look at it and remember all the good times we had and hold on to the idea that we'll be together again. If there's a way under the sun, I will find it and come back to you. We may be old and gray, but I will always, always love you."

A final kiss. And another one. And another one. Until their time was truly up. They agreed to leave from separate exits at separate times to make a clean break. And to ensure no one would see them together.

Ethan headed for the front door, looking back one last time at Liam. If he heard the horrific boom, he didn't register it until he was knocked off his feet. The last thing he could make out was smoke and fire and blood gushing down his face.

He drifted off into the inky blackness of nothing.

PART 2

CHAPTER 14

2014

HIS SHOULDER was stiff—always stiff now. Forty-three years of being a Robertson would do that to anyone. But he rolled it out and drew the bowstring back, trying to ignore his protesting left arm.

His target was in sight, thirty-five yards in front of him. The sound of his string pulled taut focused him like a laser-sight. The smell of bowstring wax and leather filled him as he breathed in and set up the shot.

Fiona was on a roll these days, sniffing out packs up and down the state and leaving no one alive in her wake. Nothing had changed much since they were kids. Fiona out on the front lines, brandishing large, short-range weapons like machetes, and Ethan, the expert sniper. But where Fiona went looking for a fight, Ethan only retaliated when provoked.

Their team had grown over the years. Men and women from all walks of life, wishing to join the fight, those seeking revenge for fallen friends and family, newfound family and new additions to the family. But Fiona's sadistic tendencies stopped her from becoming a truly great leader. He sometimes wondered if she had so many followers only because they were too scared of what she would do if they didn't follow her.

Ethan should have been happier. He was fulfilling his destiny as a Robertson. But he was scarred in new and interesting places, and every so often, something twinged that never had before, and it only served to remind him that he didn't even know what he was fighting for anymore. And after that nasty warehouse explosion twenty-three years before, the one that had almost killed him, he wondered if not running away the day he got out of the hospital had been the worst mistake he'd ever made.

He had only vague memories of the explosion. He awoke four days later, alone in the hospital. The doctor had said he would be fine, barring a few permanent scars, but he'd probably never recover the months of lost memories.

He didn't even remember his father dying at the hands of a wolf. Fiona eventually filled him in on the details—unprovoked attacks by wolves, thinning out their numbers, and how Ethan went to the warehouse on a hunch to find and kill the wolf that had killed Charles but, unfortunately, succumbed to one of their deadly traps. It was a crude, primitive method, the explosives, but it had worked.

Months of physical therapy followed, and Fiona was right there by his side, making sure he got to every appointment.

A generous trust fund had saved them from having to move to Boca with their grandparents, but staying was preventing Fiona from healing emotionally.

He could not stand to see his baby sister have the frequent panic attacks when she passed by their father's bedroom. She would glance toward his office and start crying. It killed Ethan to sell his childhood home, but he and Fiona settled nicely about 150 miles north, where there were long stretches of fields and forests to keep honing their skills. Neither had been back to their hometown in over twenty years.

He had moved for her, for his sister, because she was a lifesaver in the months that followed the accident, and she needed him to be one too, but still, there was a nagging in the back of his head, telling him he had left something far greater, far more important than his memory, there that day.

A BORED sort of noise from his right killed his focus on the target. He turned to face the source of the noise, and big blue eyes threatened to roll out of the head they were attached to. He blinked hard and sighed, relaxing the string so he could return the arrow to its quiver and rest his bow against a pole.

"Kathryn. Eleanor. Robertson. We've been out here twenty minutes. And you're already texting?" Ethan harrumphed and looked to the sky in exasperation.

Katie, the latest heir in the noble Robertson line, all of fourteen, with her mom's curls, Ethan's eyes, and her aunt Fiona's deadly aim, had slung her own bow across her chest in favor of her phone.

They were at the outdoor archery range on the far side of the outdoor multisport facility Ethan had founded when he was thirty, about forty minutes out of town. It had become the premiere destination for not only hunters to practice their skills safely, but for regular sportsmen and women just wanting to learn to shoot or hunt the regular, nonsupernatural way. It had grown into a major part of the landscape, having added designated fishing spots and camping grounds. It also afforded Ethan the freedom to attend to Robertson matters when he needed to.

"It's Saturday, *Dad*! Everyone else I know in the whole world is at the mall right now, and I'm in the middle of nowhere target-shooting. And I'm so *hungry*. Mom was all fiber! Protein! Healthy! Can't we just sneak out and go get some pancakes?" She opened her eyes wide to use that look that no dad can say no to when it comes from his daughter.

Especially when there was a chance to sneak some real, good food instead of the bland menu that was his board-certified nutritionist wife Moira's latest healthy superfood obsession.

Ethan sighed and placed his hands on Katie's shoulders with every intention of lecturing his youngest heir on the importance of training and being ready for anything, but his stomach betrayed him by growling loudly. Katie knew when she had defeated him, a trait she'd inherited from the women on both sides.

"Fine," he spat out in mock disgust.

Katie fist pumped and hissed out a victorious, "Yesssssss!"

"But—"

"No buts, Dad!" She had already dismantled her bow. If only she worked this fast during training.

"We have to—"

Katie stomped her foot, but to Ethan she just looked adorable. "Dad! Come on! No one has to know. We'll tell Aunt Fi that I snapped my string or something. I won't even tell Mom that you had *senseless carbs*."

Battle fought. Battle lost.

Spoils of war: pancakes.

It was Saturday. It should have been a pancake day anyway.

"And then you can drop me at the mall."

Utter defeat.

He sighed again and dismantled his own bow. But secretly, a normal day with his daughter was all he wanted right now. Fiona had been so aggressive lately, almost willing new battles at every turn. And she had become so stubborn, so much like Charles, that she'd tried to take on too much by herself, and it was a wonder she was not dead yet. Or that she hadn't gotten Ethan killed in the crossfire.

He was torn between Robertson loyalty and wanting to take his family and go so far away no one would ever find them, like so many former allies had done to get away from Fiona.

Between bites of chocolate chip pancakes soaked in butter and syrup, Katie casually dropped a bomb of new information on him. "So, Aunt Fi is leaving tonight on a hunt. I overheard her talking to Mom about it. Why aren't you going?"

He never wanted to play sides with his kids, but Katie was definitely a daddy's girl with a healthy sense of right and wrong.

"She's wh—did she say why? Where?" This was the first he had heard about it.

"Something about a string of mutilated bodies. I think I heard her say something about a place called Bone Valley? She didn't sound happy about it."

Bone Valley. The old phosphate mines on the edge of... *home*. She couldn't go alone after all this time trying to forget it existed.

Ethan tried to play it off casually. "Hmmmm.... Thanks for telling me, Katie."

"Dad! You can't tell her I told you! I'm not supposed to eavesdrop!" Beyond teenaged mortification, she looked—she looked scared. Katie was notorious for putting her nose into things that were none of her business, and it had gotten her grounded before, but the look on her face, the inflection in her voice....

Ethan rubbed at his temples and wondered just what kind of fear Fiona had put into his family.

"Don't worry, baby. I won't." He reached over and ruffled her hair before reaching for the check.

"Jamie's going."

Ethan slammed his coffee cup down. "What?" Once again, as with all things Fiona, remaining calm was a Herculean task.

Katie looked like she had revealed something she wasn't supposed to. "Aunt Fi said it was—"

"Oh, Aunt Fi is forgetting just whose kids you and Jamie are again." She was *not* taking his teenage son on a hunt without him. "Come on, sweetie. I need to have a talk with my sister."

Katie protested the entire way home, whining that she didn't want to get into any trouble, but, thankfully for her, no one expected Ethan and Katie to come home so early and Katie's role never had the chance to come up.

The plan—the plan *Fiona* had insisted on—was for them to be home much later in the afternoon. She had strongly suggested he take Katie to work on her bow skills. She had played up the benefits of getting to spend one-on-one time with Katie. She was parked in his driveway with hunting gear in the back and Jamie's duffel bag sitting on the tailgate.

Fiona had the decency to look surprised to see her big brother come barreling toward her. "Ethan, I—"

"Going somewhere, Fi? Taking my son with you?" She backed up with every step he took toward her.

"It's nothing, Ethan. Small beer. In-and-out kind of thing. I thought maybe I'd take Jamie and give you a br—"

"Without asking me? Where are you going, Fi? Hmmm? And before you play all coy and give me the runaround, it would do you well to remember just whose son you are taking with you."

Fiona rolled her eyes and blew out in a huff. "Jesus, Ethan! He's eighteen! Hardly a kid anymore! And he's—"

"Still living under *my* roof, Fiona. And he's still *my* son. So let's try that again. *Where are you going?*" She might have assumed the role of leader by default, but she was still his bratty little sister, he had several inches on her, and he was running out of patience more and more with her those days.

And she knew it.

"Home, all right? Home. Bunch of bodies in Bone Valley, just dumped there, and no one knows why. The whole area has been quiet since—for a long time—and there have been six deaths in the last week. And five more are missing. Some contacts called me because they think a new pack or some witch coven has breezed into town, and they asked for help, okay? It's no big deal. Nothing I can't handle. Just going to check the woodlands for activity and contain it."

He breathed in and balled his fist by her face, but instead of solving this *her* way, with violence, he instead shook his fist and pointed an accusing finger at her. "I'm—Okay, Fiona. Fine. Go home. I'm going with you."

She recoiled as if she had been bitten. "No, you're not!"

"I go with you, or I go by myself and you never get your niece and nephew alone again. How *dare* you presume to tell me what I can and can't do?" Covens were never an "in-and-out" kind of thing, and they both knew it.

"Fuck! Ethan! Look at yourself! You're not what you once were, and we all know it! Ethan, you're great from a distance when I need backup, but you've been off your game, and I need someone who can pull the trigger up close in a heartbeat, and let's face it, that's not you. That's never been you."

"Why? Because I only kill when provoked? I don't go looking for a kill?"

It struck a nerve, but addressing it proved his point and they both knew it.

She closed her eyes and pursed her lips. "Fine. Fine, Ethan. You win. But you stay in the shadows, ready to back my play, or so help me God, I will take you down at the first sign you are endangering the rest of us." Just like Charles. More and more every day.

He smiled sweetly down at Fiona. "You'll be out before the bullet leaves the chamber, dear baby sister." He backed away from her and quirked his eyebrow up. "No one threatens me. Not even you." He shrugged his shoulders before he turned away, letting her know he didn't consider her a threat. "We'll leave in an hour. I'll just go and pack my things."

Ethan should have been excited. Covens were rare and old school, but nasty business. They were a common enemy of human and wolf alike that, in an ideal world, would bring the two groups together to fight off. Few covens had ever been taken down fully over the years by hunters or packs. Those lucky enough to catch a witch could never get much useful information out of them. Even Wiccan allies proved useless in infiltrating their ranks. The chance to fight a coven should have been an honorable challenge for any Robertson worth his or her name, but Ethan halfheartedly threw some stuff in a duffel bag and, instead of mentally preparing himself for what would surely be an exciting and dangerous night, wondered how normal siblings settled their differences.

SNEAKING AN unhealthy second breakfast with Katie was a good thought he held on to later on that night when he was delivered a mighty blow to the stomach from a wolf he never had the pleasure of fighting before. Ethan fell to the ground, landing on the rough, rocky ground with a yelp.

The guy was strong, and it took everything Ethan had not to let on just how much pain he was in. The wolf was on top of him, half-turned, straddling his legs to keep him down, and he'd raised his fist for another round of blows when the sound of an arrow flying distracted them both a split second before it ripped through the man's raised hand.

The man howled in protest, and through swollen eyes, Ethan saw Jamie pull the bloodied wolf off him while Fiona stood in the distance, crossbow again at the ready.

The man freed himself from Jamie's grip easily and cradled his left hand as he turned to run. Something stopped him, though, and Ethan struggled to sit up to figure out what it could be.

The wolf was looking at his sister, who was wide-eyed and frozen, looking back at the wolf. Even from yards away, Ethan could clearly see the bow shake, and for the first time in a very long time, Fiona was *terrified*.

He shot a confused look back at Ethan, blue eyes flashing briefly in the moonlight, his eyebrows knitted together as he looked him up and down for a brief second before turning back to Fiona.

"What are you waiting for, Aunt Fi?" But his son's voice sounded a thousand miles away then.

Something, *something*, in the back of his mind put nothing and nothing together somehow, and there was a name racing through his brain.

"Liam?"

He didn't mean to open his mouth, but the wolf whipped back round to Ethan and growled. Fiona regained her composure, and another arrow went flying, this time hitting him in the shoulder.

Before Ethan could say anything else, the wolf took off at full speed deeper into the forest, and Ethan tried to stand, but in an instant, his world went black.

CHAPTER 15

SOMEONE WAS on Ethan in the space of a heartbeat, someone with dark blue eyes and gangly limbs, forcing him to stay down, pinning him there with what was probably more force than necessary. Ethan gasped for breath underneath him, his whole body tense under the weight of muscle and bone grinding into him.

Liam.

Liam... but he was younger, skinnier, his hair dark and messy.

"You never learn, do you?" Liam growled out like he was going to break at any second. He forced a knee between Ethan's legs and shoved his wrists together above his head, daring Ethan to try to struggle.

Ethan grinned wide and stared him down with unwavering eyes, like, challenge accepted, wolf.

"Then teach me."

*Ethan let his head fall back on the soft earth—*I think I'm in Cocoa. How did I get to Cocoa? I haven't been here for years.*—and Liam pressed in close for a messy kiss, like a desperate, basic need, more important than air or water or food, or that Ethan's lips alone could have taken the place of all of them and he would have been just fine. Ethan gave back exactly what he got, making the best use of his mouth and tongue because the rest of him was deliciously restrained.*

"How can I when you keep looking at me like that?" He knew Liam could feel the hard line in Ethan's jeans, and it was the best way to let Liam know he had officially lost what little control he'd ever had of the situation.

Ethan opened his eyes wide in mock innocence and bit his lip like he didn't know exactly what that did to people. To Liam.

"Think of it as good practice for you too. There's not much difference between me distracting you like this and, say, a vampire's spell." He tilted his head back more, exposing his neck, something Liam could never resist.

Liam tried to look annoyed and failed at it miserably. "Except I'm trying to tutor you in early Christian practices of Medieval Europe and not supernatural self-defense. And vampires don't actually exist."

Ethan laughed softly and jerked his hips up into Liam, letting him know in no uncertain terms that World History was history and he needed to focus on the present situation in his jeans.

Liam sighed and rolled his eyes, like fucking Ethan was a huge inconvenience, but they both knew it wasn't true.

"C'mon, Liam. I can't focus like this. And my test is Tuesday. I have to pass this class with at least a B to keep my scholarship, you know that." Ethan grabbed Liam's hand and guided it to his erection just in case he'd forgotten in the last second that it was there.

Liam traced the outline of it teasingly. "Will you promise to focus afterward? And I mean really focus? Nothing but study, study, study until it's time to leave?"

"I promise. I'll know more about Charlemagne than his own mother did by the time we leave today." He doubted that, and the look on Liam's face showed he doubted that too, but it didn't stop Liam from sitting up to unzip Ethan's jeans.

The moment his mouth wrapped around Ethan, ready to get him off so he could finally just *pay attention*, was the moment Ethan woke up—older, alone, in the dark, confused, in a lot of pain, and very hard. A vague sense of profound loss he couldn't explain was quickly falling away, retreating back to the deepest parts of his mind, and he couldn't recall it to make sense of it.

He sat up in bed and rubbed at his eyes. He vaguely remembered taking that class in college, must have passed it because he had maintained his scholarship. He remembered Cocoa and many weekend and day trips there, even remembered the spot he was at in the dream. There was a familiarity to everything he saw.

Save Liam.

Liam Kinnaird. The name popped into his head. It all made sense now… or, actually, it didn't make any sense at all.

What was *that* all about? Ethan and Liam had never been friends, much less friendly enough to… he'd never even seen Liam until the previous night. Or had he? *How did I know his name?*

Must be the stress. Yes. The stress of everything. That must have been it.

Maybe they'd crossed paths once and he'd forgotten. He had forgotten a lot. Maybe they'd fought before. They certainly didn't— they weren't—they couldn't have been….

Ethan shook himself more awake. He was alone in the guest bedroom. Moira hated when he came home all bloodied. She'd rather toss second-rate guest sheets than try to clean blood out of the nice five-billion-thread-count sheets on their bed. He must have been more injured than he thought to be out for the hours-long drive back home. Not exactly a testament to his usefulness.

But other thoughts took precedence right then.

Fighting, fucking, they were not so different, were they? Both adrenaline-fueled, intense events. Hatred, lust, both intense emotions. Maybe he had a concussion and neurons were misfiring or *something* because there was no way he and a Kinnaird would ever, ever be together, even if it didn't exactly feel like just a dream….

That thought saw him through his orgasm when his erection refused to go away on its own. Conflicting thoughts of killing Liam and fucking Liam merged in his head when he didn't want them to, but he couldn't chase them away as he spilled over his hand onto his belly, the Liam in his mind sucking his cock, moaning around it as Ethan spilled down his throat.

He drifted back off to sleep without bothering to clean himself up first.

CHAPTER 16

MORNING CAME and brought too-bright sunshine and the sounds and smells of Jamie making coffee downstairs. He gave Ethan the once-over, checking for any signs of a lingering concussion or any other kind of trauma before offering him a strong Cuban coffee to jolt him awake.

Ethan went about his day and didn't think about the dream at all. It was just one of those things. Nothing much surprised him anymore, and he was never one to panic about a less-than-heterosexual fantasy. Just a thing. Nothing to worry about. Fighting, fucking, love, hate, physical reactions, chemical reactions. They happened, and sometimes they got mixed up. It was human.

Days passed with dreamless nights. He had moved on, forgotten. It was not important enough to warrant further thought, though. Not when his relationship with Fiona grew colder and colder as the days went by. She hadn't called him, but he knew she had been fighting without him.

Moira and Fiona had always been close, but now his wife and his sister seemed to be against him, and they were taking Jamie along too. He had been coming home late, covered in dirt and bruises, and refused to make eye contact with Ethan.

ONE NIGHT about a week and a half later, something on the edge of his bed startled him awake. It was dark, but he could just make out a figure in the glow of his clock that read 3:23.

He opened his mouth to yell, to scare the figure, distract him until he could find a weapon, but a hand clapped over it before he could get a sound out.

"When will you ever learn? You're such a paranoid sleeper." It was barely a whisper, but there was warmth and amusement running under the urgency.

"Mmm-pmph." Liam.

"Of course, silly. Who else would be so horny that he risks his ass breaking into Charles Robertson's house to mercilessly fuck his only son in the middle of the night? Wait. Don't answer that. I don't want to know if there's someone else." He uncovered Ethan's mouth.

"There's no one else, Liam. You know that. And there never will be." God, so cheesy. But Liam sighed contentedly and pushed Ethan back down so he could stretch out on top of him.

"Is this okay? I mean, you don't have anything important going on first thing in the morning, do you?"

Ethan chuckled quietly. "Just a huge presentation in my lit class. No big deal. Just, like, thirty percent of my final grade."

Liam groaned but didn't make a move to get off Ethan. "Well, I should let you sleep, then. Thirty percent, right? You need to be in tip-top shape f—"

Ethan shut Liam up with a kiss, and when he melted into it, Ethan knew he'd won.

Ethan managed to stay quiet as Liam swallowed his cock, something he should have attributed, ironically, to Charles and his insane stealth training—to kill wolves, not fuck them, but Ethan was adaptable—yet he pushed that thought away as he spilled into Liam's mouth.

They both enjoyed making the sex and the lazy cuddling that came after last as long as possible before Liam had to sneak back out into the darkness to avoid the early rising Charles. Ethan would have bet any amount that there was a part of Liam that wanted to be caught.

After lying entwined until it became risky, Liam finally rose and kissed him good-bye. A promise of more lingered between them, as it always did when they parted. He dressed and climbed out the window, leaving Ethan satisfied, but alone again.

He closed his eyes and drifted back to sleep.

He awakened, again, and looked at the clock. It was barely 2:00 a.m., and it took him a moment to realize that it was not 1991 and he was not twenty years old and he was definitely not having sex with Liam.

But he *was* definitely hard again. And there was that same sense of loss and longing he couldn't figure out.

He tried to think of anyone but Liam as he grabbed his cock, thrusting up into his fist, but the dreams seemed so real, he could almost feel the remnants of Liam's touch on his skin. He recalled the look on Liam's face as he came in his dream, how he struggled to stay quiet as Liam reached between them to take Ethan in his hand and make him come as well.

He was so incredibly hard, and Moira was sleeping quietly next to him, but for some reason, the thought of waking her up and making love to her didn't seem right.

He made his way to the bathroom and came quicker and harder than he had in a long time and deliberately did not think about what that meant, what any of this meant. Because he was not sure he wanted to get to the bottom of it. He might not like what he would find there.

He threw himself into his work, into hunting and training in his off hours, and readying people for what would surely escalate into a full-on war thanks to Fiona channeling Charles more and more.

Closer to home, there were still battles to fight. A new pack had blown into town. They were young and reckless. Fortunately for the Robertsons, not all packs were descendants of the Kinnairds. Made wolves—ones that did not have Kinnaird blood in their veins even if made by a Kinnaird—were not protected by the treaty. The rules did not apply to them. And these wolves were easy enough to spot, even from a distance, with a little training. They were rarely successful, well-organized, or long-lived, but they did tend to leave a high body count before they were contained.

They made an attempt on a random girl at the local college. They tried and failed, but it pushed the berserk button of Fiona's best hunter, Antonio, and he tore a path through the forest, managing to kill at least two by himself.

Ethan halfheartedly wondered if Antonio would do the same if it were Fiona or Katie or even himself, but on a routine patrol—*is that all*

I'm good for?—on his own the next day, everything became crystal clear when he silently stumbled upon the pair in the remotest part of the woods. The girl, Sasha—not so randomly chosen by the pack it seemed—was pushed against a tree, her legs wrapped around Antonio's mostly naked form, bodies pushing and pulling in perfect rhythm with each other as Antonio slowly fucked her.

Ethan felt perverted watching them, but he couldn't find the strength to look away. He wouldn't risk getting closer to hear what they were saying to each other, but from the way Antonio curled protectively around Sasha's entire body, it was obvious the attempt on her terrified him.

He should have looked away. This was a private moment and there was no need to intrude on it, but they were beautiful together and obviously in love. Sasha was flushed from the forehead down, and she closed her eyes as her lips parted in a small *O* of pleasure.

He should have gone while they were distracted. He should have walked away and forgotten what he saw, but from above the din of the forest, Sasha cried out Antonio's name and went limp in his arms, and Ethan was so hard watching them fuck like this in secret, he wouldn't have been able to walk anyway.

Antonio's voice got louder the closer to his orgasm he got. Ethan could just about make out what he was saying then, talking of how he'd almost lost her and "never letting you out of my sight again, Sasha. Never. Tried to protect you. I thought if…I thought no one would ever find out and you'd be safe. I'm sorry, Sasha. I'm sorry."

It got difficult to make out again. Suddenly Antonio threw his head back and growled and came inside Sasha, and those odd, unexplainable feelings again came roaring to the front of Ethan's mind, and suddenly he didn't feel guilty or perverted as much as he felt sad and grieving for something he couldn't quite put his finger on. He kept her secret to keep her safe. Why could Ethan relate to that feeling of secrecy, of possession, of crippling fear of being found out?

He gathered himself and retreated before either of them could notice he was there.

The next time he dreamed, that very night, there was no pretense, no doubt that he was dreaming.

He had Liam up against a wall in a no-tell motel room, his body pinned to the door, and he shoved Liam's jeans down and fell to the floor with them, hungrily taking Liam's cock in his mouth while Liam groaned and tugged at Ethan's hair, pushing him, pulling him closer, greedy for more, and Ethan just wanted to give, give, give.

"Jesus, Ethan, you were really worried...."

Ethan didn't respond, just took more of him in and wrapped his arms around Liam's torso until Liam pulled him back to standing. Liam's eyes were dark and concerned, a faint smear of blood colored his chin, and Ethan wanted to take away any lingering pain he might still be feeling.

He surged forward and kissed Liam violently, unable to stop himself even when Liam tried to slow him down.

"I almost lost you, Liam. My own people almost killed you. Don't ask me to stop. Don't make me stop. I can't, not when I almost saw you die."

"I wasn't—" Ethan cut him off with another kiss. Liam pushed him off and held his face between his hands to still him. "I wasn't. I know you need this. You're not going to get rid of me that easily, okay? I don't plan on dying at the hands of a human."

Liam rested his forehead on Ethan's and closed his eyes. Ethan felt his whole body relax into his touch, and he pressed close, feeling Liam breathe against him until he was calm enough to think clearly again.

Liam let Ethan guide him to the bed, let him do what he needed to get through the night. Ethan rutted against him roughly, biting and digging his short nails into his skin. He needed to mark him, claim him even if just for the moment until the marks started to heal. He pulled him in like he needed every inch of them touching, and Liam didn't protest, just curled into him and didn't censor the needy, desperate noises tumbling from his lips.

Ethan rutted harder, faster, and selfish, insane thoughts spun around his head that convinced him Liam was his and no one else's. No one else should give Liam such intense emotions like pain and suffering and joy and ecstasy. Each thrust against Liam brought a new surge of possession, of dangerous obsession and greed, and he would have absolutely, right then, without a second thought, killed anyone who got in the way. Human hunters, friends, Charles, Fiona....

He came loudly, spilling on Liam, gripping him tightly as he pumped Liam's cock in his fist so he joined soon after. When he had the strength, he flipped Liam and crawled back on top of him, ran his hands on all the skin he could find, kissed every inch of him like he would never get another chance.

"You're mine, Liam. Mine." He said it over and over again until....

He opened his eyes and sighed when he realized he'd been dreaming again. He noted with mild amusement that he didn't need to worry about jerking off since he'd already come on himself in his sleep.

CHAPTER 17

ONCE HE could dismiss. Twice he could ignore. Three times and there was something going on. He needed answers.

Fiona had been steadfastly ignoring him since the forest. He called, texted, even went to her apartment, but when Fiona didn't want to be found, she wouldn't be found. But the time for politeness and patience was up.

Who is Liam? He hit send and waited.

Twenty minutes passed before his phone chirped.

No one. Nothing. Another monster to kill.

Lies, lies, and lies.

He tried again. *He certainly seemed to know you.*

This time the response came within thirty seconds.

He's no one. END OF STORY.

So much missing from the time before the explosion. He must have known him then. He could just maybe make out—yeah, there was a fight. A big one. He could see Fiona crying, hear her screaming, and…. Was Liam there? There was something strangely familiar about the fight that night in the woods outside Bone Valley.

Nothing? Is that really going to be your story?

Leave it alone, Ethan. This isn't your fight.

He shook his head in disbelief and swiped across her name on his phone to call her. She picked up immediately.

"Isn't my fight—the fuck, Fi? *I knew his name.*" His fist curled at his side.

"God*damn* it, Ethan! Why can't you ever just follow a fucking order?"

"This isn't about following orders, Fi! You've been sketchy and secretive ever since I got out of the hospital. I've been patient for *twenty years* waiting for you to help fill in the gaps in my memory, and you've not volunteered one bit of helpful information in that time. I know there's something you don't want me remembering. I've known it for over twenty years. Something happened, and I know I'll never get it out of you. But you know what I think? I think this guy knows. That's why you froze when you saw his face. That's how I know his name. I think I'm going to go to him and get some of my memories back."

He could hear Fiona screaming threats at him if he tried as he pulled the phone away to disconnect the call.

He wondered how normal people with nine-to-five jobs dealt with things as he packed an overnight bag and some weapons, threw them in the back of his truck, and made the three-plus-hour trip south without a second thought.

Searching the forests of his childhood for the man he was both trying to kill and dreaming erotically about wasn't one of his smarter ideas, but if there was one thing he had learned in his forty-odd years, it was that nothing was ever a coincidence when it came to the supernatural.

Ethan knew he needed a plan that would somehow entice the man and the wolf inside him if he didn't want to be at this for days.

No one had ever accused Ethan of having well-thought-out plans and this one was no different. He rolled his head around to crack his stiff neck, resigning himself to another night in the guest room. He pulled out his sharpest knife and went to work on himself, making small superficial cuts that ensured that his blood would spill on the forest floor, that the scent would carry and cover a wider path than he could alone in twice the time.

He prayed he could handle any other creature that might pick up on his scent too. He packed his quiver with his most damaging crossbow bolts just in case.

Ethan leaned against a tree, nursing his wounds as best he could in the field. He'd jammed his over shirt against the cuts to let the blood soak into the fabric, giving him another layer of the scent. He knew Liam knew the smell. He'd bled pretty badly that night with Fiona. He hoped Liam would catch it now and come right to him.

The cuts may have been shallow, but they still stung and burned when the fabric of his clothes stuck to the drying blood on his skin. The pain gave him a kind of hyperawareness, though, and he could sense the moment Liam stepped behind a tall, thick pine tree to watch Ethan.

Ethan didn't speak. The next move was Liam's to make.

Ethan could only see his face from behind the tree. Liam's lip curled, and Ethan had fought too many wolves in his life not to recognize the look of a man seriously considering his wolf's desire to see Ethan's insides hang from the branches and the look of a wolf seriously considering his human's desire to stay calm.

Liam didn't move from behind the tree. All he said, teeth bared and claws out, breath harsh in his lungs like he was trying to contain a tidal wave, was one word that would satisfy them both.

"Run."

Ethan looked up at Liam. His fingers scraped the bark of the pine trees, dug in hard as pieces broke off and fell to the ground. He straightened up despite the pain, breathed in sharply, and gave him his answer.

"No."

Ethan's heart pounded against his ribs, but he was not going to run even if he didn't know if Liam was trying to warn him off or ordering him to do it so the wolf could have some fun with him.

Liam looked down at the ground and looked back up again, eyes aglow, and growled out, "I warned you, Robertson." Ethan didn't know if it was a threat or a promise, and he honestly didn't know which one he wanted more.

"I'm not looking for a fight, Liam. I'm relatively unarmed. These arrows were not meant for a wolf. And I'm not going to run so you can play out some revenge on me." They both knew that, unarmed and injured, he didn't stand a chance, and Ethan had more dignity than that.

If only that were all there was to it.

"Revenge? For what? For that little skirmish? Pretty sure I've survived worse than an arrow to the hand. This is so not revenge. You come into my forest. Hunt. Get your blood and your scent everywhere. Did you not think about this before you let yourself get hurt? Leaving a trail for me to find, for the wolf to find. What did you think would happen out here?" Liam still hadn't moved from behind the tree.

"Exactly what I would want to happen, Liam." Ethan released his stomach, lifted up his shirt, and tossed it aside to reveal the shallow, self-inflicted flesh wounds. Liam narrowed his eyes and stumbled a bit against the tree.

Why won't he come at me?

The realization that Ethan wasn't hunting for just something, he was hunting for him, crept across Liam's face, and Ethan would have smiled if he didn't know just how dangerous that would be.

Liam didn't say a word in response, though. He looked defeated and bewildered, and Ethan couldn't help but feel like, in some sick way, they were flirting.

More than just flirting, negotiating for how this was going to happen, how it would all go down. And God help him for that word choice. Even in his own mind, it heated his skin and did something to the air between them that made him part his lips.

"Something on your mind?" Ethan cocked his head to the side because he already knew the answer.

Liam's mouth tightened into a thin line and he glared at Ethan. "You. Like you didn't know. Smelling like that. I don't know what's stronger—your blood or your fear." Liam winced, and it was the first indication that something was not right. "And right now, I want to taste both."

Ethan stared at him with defiant blue eyes and knew he might not have the strength of a wolf, but was stronger than Liam for making him fight his wolf like that.

"I don't want to hurt you, Ethan." His breaths were shallower and broken.

But Ethan saw right through him.

"Yes you do, Liam." The lines were drawn, the rules were set, and Ethan dropped his crossbow and raised his hands. He was completely unarmed, defenseless. *Come get me.*

Liam howled, and it wasn't one of victory or anger or rage. It was the same as the night Fiona had shot him. It was pain.

"Are you saying yes?" Liam inched around the tree, but his show of strength was waning.

"Yes to what? Beating me? Killing me? Turning me?" The drying blood pulled and stretched at the skin on his neck as he arched it... offered it, if he was being honest with himself.

"Yes to...." Liam closed his eyes and groaned. Something was definitely wrong. "To anything I want to...."

Ethan felt like he should be the one to close the gap between them, to offer help instead of initiate a fight.

Liam growled. "I won't be nice about it either. I'll make you bruise and bleed and hurt. I'm an animal, Ethan. I don't care if you die. Are you still saying yes? Do you still want to try to win?"

"Why do you keep asking me that, animal?" Ethan sneered and spat the word back at him. They both knew Liam wasn't in any condition to fight. Ethan didn't understand why Liam was still trying to get him to believe otherwise. Ethan was irritated and itching for something to happen. "Are you all talk, wolf? Or is this going somewhere?"

"Oh, Ethan." Liam grinned, but it was pained. "You have no idea where this is...."

Liam closed his eyes, longer this time. When he opened them again, they were unfocused and glazed. His eyelids looked heavy, and he swayed and stumbled until he collapsed on the forest floor.

"Liam?" Ethan picked up his crossbow and approached Liam with trepidation. Liam did not respond. The closer he got to Liam, the more pale he looked. He wasn't faking it.

"Liam?" Ethan gingerly walked around the back side of the pine tree where Liam lay unconscious.

There was blood everywhere. More than from Ethan's silly trap to lure Liam out. Liam's belly was completely red and, unlike Ethan's own cuts, the blood hadn't stopped flowing. He'd been hurt pretty badly and he wasn't healing.

Ethan sucked his teeth and looked at Liam's bleeding form for a moment before damning himself for another poorly thought-out plan.

He might not get answers, but a Robertson never turned down an opportunity.

He ensured that Liam was alive, but not so much that he would wake up, and lifted him over his shoulder. He had rudimentary first aid supplies in his truck and bandaged him up as best he could. As much as he hated the idea of cleaning blood out of his interior later, he didn't think Liam would survive the three-hour trip north in the bed of the truck and instead laid him down in the backseat. Liam stirred a few times during the trip but never fully woke up.

He was never more thankful that Moira and Katie were away for a girls' weekend with Moira's mother in Orlando, and that Jamie was practically living at his girlfriend's house these days.

He dragged a moaning Liam into the garage. There was a ratty old cot they should have dumped years ago, and Ethan was going to do just that after he was done here, but for the moment, it was the perfect place to cuff Liam so he could figure out just what was wrong with him and why he was not healing. And to figure how Ethan could duplicate this effect on Liam or any wolf, really.

Ethan knew a few spells he'd picked up from Kevin Hughes and his Wiccan family when he and Kevin were friends in high school. They were mostly weak locating spells meant for finding stray arrows in the field or, more usefully, lost car keys, and a masking spell that hid the effects of the first time Ethan tried beer when he was seventeen, but he knew of nothing that could heal Liam when he was not healing himself.

Ethan wished he could call on Kevin for help, but at some point in college, Kevin had decided fighting the good fight, or any fight really, wasn't for him. Ethan always felt a little jealous that outsiders could just pack up and leave whenever they felt it wasn't worth it anymore.

He pored over every book in the house that would help him and found nothing. Two hours later, he gave up and called in a favor with another old Wiccan friend who was thankfully neutral to both sides and knew when to be quiet about things.

Timothy Fribbs had been shunned and threatened with a long, slow death by Fiona years before after she caught him helping a small pack perform a locating spell. He'd tried to explain it was to find a lost child, but to Fiona a wolf was a wolf. Even a child deserved to die, and if he was alone and scared, all the better. Ethan didn't agree with most things Fiona did, but that one hit him harder than others. Fribbs was a good friend and a good man. He had no loyalties. He just wanted to help.

Tim picked up after the third ring.

"Fribbs, I need your help."

"Human troubles or supernatural ones?"

Ethan explained the situation as best he could without giving away too many details of the strange nature of his relationship with Liam. Not that he could if he wanted to. He didn't even know how to explain it to himself.

"Yeesh. That sounds pretty dark, Ethan. You sure you want to be messing with that kind of stuff?"

Ethan looked toward the unconscious man in his garage and made a face. "Well, it's a little late now, Fribbs. I'm in it pretty deep."

He heard Tim blow out a breath on the other end of the line. "Hmmm... I got a healing spell. It's pretty powerful and just might do the trick. But, listen, Eth, I don't want any trouble from that crazy-ass sister of yours. She's not around, is she?"

"No. We're not exactly speaking to each other right now." Saying that out loud was a relief. He would be okay never speaking to her again if only he didn't think she could tell him everything he wanted to know about his past and his connection to Liam.

Tim chuckled. "Join the club, man. Listen, I'll do this for you because I owe you, but after that, you're on your own. I don't want to get mixed up with your family again. I love you, man. You're like a brother to me and I always got your back, but I can't be dealing with Fiona if she finds out I was there. Is this worth it to you?"

"It" could mean Liam or it could mean the truth. He knew the two were linked.

"I wouldn't ask otherwise, Fribbs."

Tim sighed. "Okay. Okay, just wait for me. I'll get everything together and head over there soon, but Ethan, you gotta make sure Fiona isn't around."

After they hung up, there was nothing Ethan could do but wait. He focused on Liam's every breath, just in case they stopped.

The healing spell was intense. Ethan watched Tim in morbid fascination as he performed it. The innocent spells Kevin had taught him were nothing like this. But as Tim left him alone with a sleeping Liam so he could recover, he admitted there was no guarantee that it would work. They still had no idea what had done this to Liam, although Tim did sense a dark and very old something around him.

"Ethan, we have to find out what did this to him. My spell might hold or it might not be powerful enough against whatever did this to him. I could get a better idea if I knew what did this to him." He took a sample of the blood from the wound to help him work out what could possibly disable a werewolf so thoroughly. "I'm going to go home and try to see if I recognize anything in the blood."

Ethan nodded.

"Is it worth it trying to save this guy? Is this why you and Fiona aren't talking?"

Ethan pinched the bridge of his nose. "He knows something, Fribbs. I've been trying to wrestle the truth about my past from Fiona for years, and she isn't talking. Something is telling me this guy is connected to it."

Tim peered at Liam and turned back to Ethan with a wary look on his face. "I don't think this guy is going to talk either. He doesn't seem like the chatty type."

"If you figure out what this is, could you let me in on it?"

Tim squinted and rolled his head around. "Possibly. You going to turn around and kill him with it afterward?"

"No. But it could be useful." He tried to look as casual as he could.

"Not if it falls in the wrong hands." The unspoken word—"Fiona"—hung in the air.

"Our secret?" But the bigger secret was the ulterior motive he kept inside his head.

"I don't know what you have planned, but I think I have an idea. Ethan, I'm not a fan, but I also know that you're not Fiona. Do I have your word that you're not going to abuse it? That I can leave this guy with you and he'll be safe?"

Ethan nodded. He had no intention of killing Liam or even inflicting mortal damage. He just... he just wanted answers. And feelings aside, Ethan was trained the same way Fiona was. He knew what he was doing.

Tim was wary, but he left Ethan a copy of the spell book and a few doses of the prepared oil.

Hours passed, and Ethan checked on Liam's progress like clockwork. It was slow going, but Liam did appear to be gaining strength. His wounds had begun stitching themselves together, leaving only drying blood and raised welts.

At the four-hour mark, Ethan made his way into the garage once more, and this time he heard the slightest difference in Liam's breathing. He was awake but probably trying not to call attention to himself, though, not knowing in whose presence he found himself right then.

Ethan clicked on the light, and it was too bright for Liam. He squeezed his eyes shut like it was still burning through his eyelids and pulled on the cuffs keeping him at bay. Ethan prayed the pain was too much for him to even consider breaking them.

"You're going to live." He tried to sound flat, disinterested, but he could hear his own heartbeat, which was probably telling Liam a different story. "You're starting to heal."

Liam sighed and stopped moving. Ethan watched the defeat roll through him, and it was almost amusing. "Thanks to you, I suppose? You kept me alive when you could have finished the job."

Ethan turned the light so it shined on his wound. "I kept you alive to learn how you can be killed. Isn't that ironic? I called in a favor, and you're under a very powerful healing spell. Who did this to you?"

Layers of cotton gauze stuck to his skin, and Ethan wasn't gentle in pulling it back to examine him.

Liam breathed in sharply, wincing at the sudden increase in pain. "Why should I tell you?" He gritted his teeth as if trying to get the words out, to sound tougher than he must feel.

Ethan leaned in close, inches from his face, and pressed a thumb in on the slowly healing flesh, making Liam arch up painfully and cry out. Ethan's heart pounded in his ears. "Because if you don't, I'll just let you die, and we'll figure it out anyway as we tear your corpse apart." No good ever came from showing emotion in a situation like this. Liam wouldn't talk if he sensed Ethan was weak. Fiona may have been a psycho, but she was a damned good psycho who knew how to get people to talk when she wanted them to. He channeled some of that unrelenting cruelty Charles had tried to instill in both of them. Ethan had the upper hand fully now, and he wasn't going to let go until he got some answers.

Hot breath on his face and still Liam shivered. In an instant the moment was over and Ethan's thumb pulled away, giving Liam a brief moment of relief. Ethan smiled unnervingly. He riffled through the first aid supplies, found the antibiotic, and dabbed some of the stinging liquid on Liam until he hissed.

"Don't want you to get an infection, do we?"

Liam should have been somewhat comforted by the smell of antiseptic. It was not poison or acid or magic. He tried to look down to see just how bad it was, but the moment he managed to lift his head, Ethan slammed him back down on the lumpy pillow.

"Now, what did this?"

Liam sighed. "A witch." Like it wasn't obvious. Like he thought there were no other things that could take him down at that point.

Ethan snorted. "Magic. Of course. A curse that slows healing. Or stops it altogether." Nothing he didn't already suspect, but he wouldn't give that away. He quirked his eyebrow. His physical reaction was the only thing belying his feigned disinterest. "Could be useful."

"Also, if you cared, it's a witch from the same coven that is leaving those bodies around. Your sister is so determined to pin that on my kind."

Funny how Ethan believed Liam over his own sister, but he was not going to give that away either.

"How did one get so close without you knowing it?"

Liam looked as offended as he possibly could in his condition. "If you must know, I've been a little off my game lately. Bitch was on me before I knew it. All words and black powder and suddenly a long knife going right through me. Their funny idea to make death as slow as possible."

Ethan nodded but said nothing.

He redressed the injury with focused precision and little pain. He remained silent while he tore into sterile gauze packages and ripped tape. Liam seemed almost impressed by the skill Ethan displayed tending to him.

Ethan cradled Liam's head in one arm and offered him lukewarm water. Liam choked a little as it leaked from his lips, mixing with dried blood as it trickled down his chin. When he'd had his fill, Ethan slid his arm from under his head, letting it rest on the pillow again.

"Are you comfortable?"

Liam was fading, his eyelids were drooping. Ethan figured he'd lost a lot of blood. He was cold to the touch, and before Ethan could think to ask if he needed a blanket, Liam passed out.

Ethan stared at his sleeping form for a long time, wondering if he was about to do the right thing. He called Tim with the confirmation that it was a witch with some kind of black powder.

"Well, that's good news on all fronts, I guess. I think I've figured out the spell. Nasty one, too. Old, but actually pretty basic. The combination of plants and metals is like nothing I've ever seen before. But the healing spell I did is good against it. Are—are you sure you want to do this still?"

Ethan was not sure of anything anymore, but he'd come too far to turn around. This could be his only chance to make sense of the mess in his life. "I'm sure."

"Okay, I'm going to drop it off, but I'm not coming inside. This is where I get off this crazy train."

"Thanks, Tim. I promise that I won't do anything stupid, okay?"

Tim sounded wary. "I hope not."

Ethan hung up and checked on Liam again.

LIAM SLEPT for another hour and a half, leaving Ethan time to prepare, just in case. It was near dinner when he heard a faint voice calling out from the garage. He took a deep breath and whispered over and over that it was for the greater good.

Ethan covered Liam's eyes this time as the light at his bedside flicked on. He traced the outline of the cuffs at his wrists, willing his body to stay calm and his mind to stay strong.

"I can take these off. Let you rest comfortably until you are healed." Ethan removed his hand from Liam's eyes. "Or I can shove you in a silver cage and watch you squirm. It's your call."

It was not a generous offer, and they both knew it. "What do I have to do?"

He smiled again, no less unnerving. "It's quite simple, Liam. I've been researching the spell with someone experienced in magic, and we think we've identified it. Luckily for you, I think I've identified the counterspell as well."

Ethan pressed his fingers into the wound, knowing it had healed enough so touching it wasn't excruciatingly painful like it had been just a few hours before. Liam breathed out shakily. "It's too important to just let go, and I think at this point you owe me one."

Liam rolled his eyes. "You're going to try to cast the spell on me again."

"That's the idea, yeah."

Liam's skin didn't rip when Ethan peeled the gauze away this time. Ethan allowed him a look, and it was angry red still, but it was *healed*. Ethan ran his finger along it slowly, the bumps and welts of newly stitched skin ultrasensitive under his touch. He noticed Liam breathing faster and the slight shiver in his abdomen, but he didn't give that fact away.

"Don't worry, Liam. I won't hurt you this badly. I took you in. Against my better judgment. But you are in my care, and no matter how I feel about you, the rules dictate just how far I can go with you."

"So you get to cast the spell on me and then hurt me some more before you try to heal me." Liam raised an eyebrow. "Why do I get the feeling this deal is going to be grossly one-sided? If I agree...."

Ethan warmed up some salve between his fingers, never taking his eyes off Liam. Liam sucked in his belly involuntarily when he moved to rub it on. Ethan jerked his fingers away quickly in protest and surrender. "Relax. Just lavender and rose extract. It's not all magic and supernatural. It's actually my daughter's. Got it from the mall or something, but it'll soothe those red marks you still have."

Liam seemed satisfied with the explanation, and he let Ethan apply the balm. Once again, Ethan used great care and precision and an almost *tenderness*, fingertips just brushing over Liam's skin. If Liam's fingertips were curled into his palms, absentmindedly pulling at the restraints because some part of him needed to respond to that light touch, well, Ethan chalked it up to the lingering dark magic at work inside him.

Liam had to see what was going on, had to know Ethan was hiding something under the tough exterior. Even Ethan could hear his own body reacting. "If you agree, you can rest off the effects of the healing spell comfortably. No restraints. A comfortable bed. And when you feel ready? You can leave. If you don't agree, I do it anyway and you heal right here in the dark, tied up until I see fit to release you."

"And who's to say I won't kill you when I'm healed?" But Liam's voice was too shaky to sound threatening.

Ethan leaned in close, his voice low and dangerous. "I saved your life. I saved your life when I should have let you die on the forest floor. And all I ask in return is this one tiny favor—"

"You want me to help you find a way to kill my kind. That's not a tiny favor." Point taken. But still....

"If I recall, wolves have gone after each other in the past. Who's to say the knowledge wouldn't benefit you too?" A good question. He hoped Liam saw it the same way.

Liam swallowed thickly and nodded in reluctant agreement. "Fine. Fine. Do it. Do it and get it over with." He turned his head away from Ethan, and if he was listening for any change in his heartbeat,

Ethan was pretty sure even the people next door could have heard it soaring.

Gun to Liam's back, Ethan let him take care of his bathroom needs and eat a bit. It was nothing special, rare burgers, but he looked stronger at least with the protein in his system.

Liam stretched, his eyes focused on how his skin pulled at the little mark that remained. He touched it, looked at it in the mirror, and Ethan knew Liam felt the hot intensity of being stared at as he moved. He knew Liam knew Ethan was watching him, knew Ethan wasn't immune to what he was seeing.

There was a pair of clean sweatpants waiting on the counter for him, a small gift from Ethan to prove he would make him as comfortable as possible if he just behaved.

"I've got...." Ethan trailed off when Liam shrugged out of the jeans, leaving him naked and unashamed. He didn't turn and look at Ethan as he took his time putting on the sweats, and when he did get them on, he let them hang low on his hips, and Ethan wasn't breathing. "Got everything ready for the spell and the counterspell. Looks pretty good—uh, easy."

Liam turned around. "And why can't your friend do it? Isn't he the expert here? Tell me, Ethan, have you ever practiced any kind of magic before, or do I stand a chance of coming out of this with three heads?"

Ethan stood and walked to Liam, backing him up against the counter. "Because this is mine. My catch. My rules."

Liam breathed in. "I'm beginning to get that."

Ethan knitted his eyebrows together in confusion for a moment but composed himself just as quickly. "Let's get started." He raised the gun and motioned with it for Liam to walk out of the bathroom.

Liam threw up his hands in a show of peace. "You don't need that, you know. I said yes."

He shoved the cold metal to Liam's ribs. "I have trust issues."

"You going to use that on me in a minute anyway?"

Ethan narrowed his eyes, a bit taken aback at the accusation. He loosened his grip on the pistol. "I'm not cruel, Liam."

Liam merely shrugged. "We'll see, won't we?"

Back to the hard, lumpy bed in the garage, the cuffs, and the promise of more pain to come. The restraints clicked into place around Liam's wrists and ankles, and the ritual began. Flurries of Gaelic flew as Ethan read from the unfolded piece of paper Tim had left along with the black smelly powder. The moment he sprinkled the black powder on him, Ethan saw the weakness rush over Liam once again. Liam pulled at the restraints in something Ethan might have called fear or helplessness, but he kept reading. He recited louder and louder until he reached the end and the last of the powder slipped from his fingers onto Liam's chest. Liam seemed unable to keep his eyes open.

Out of breath from concentration, Ethan dropped the paper on the bedside table and cupped Liam's face. "Open your eyes."

Liam obliged and moaned a little, but it was drowned out by Ethan's heart beating out something that felt like relief.

"How do you feel?" *God, what am I doing?*

"Weak." *Human.* "Like I did before."

Ethan held up a knife. It was not special or magical or even very large, but it was sharp and going to hurt. It was the most humane way to tell if the spell had worked. "I *am* sorry about this, if it's any consolation."

Liam could only nod.

Sorry can only get a man so far, though, when his body tells a different story. Ethan slid the flat side of the blade across Liam's stomach, and he did not miss the little moan that escaped Liam's lips the moment the cold metal touched his skin. Ethan cocked his head to the side and raised an eyebrow, but that's all the reaction he let himself have then.

He traced along the path of the original cut with the point, only letting it scratch the tiniest bit at the end, and he watched Liam for a reaction. Liam looked away from Ethan's face and focused on the knife, where it went and what it did to his skin.

In for a penny, in for a pound now, and Liam's reactions were fascinating. Ethan ran it over a nipple, the dull edge catching so slightly against it. Liam bit his lip as if to stifle his response. It didn't stop Ethan from finding the other nipple and repeating the move on it, breathing harder himself.

The blade moved up his collarbone and settled at Liam's neck, the artery throbbing against the metal.

"I could hurt you here. Watch you bleed out for a while. But you trust me, don't you, Liam? Trust that I'll stick to the rules and do the right thing?" He smiled widely. "I guess you *have* to trust me right now."

He pushed the knife in slightly, but moved it just as quickly before it did any damage.

"I don't suppose you're going to tell me how we know each other?"

Liam looked up from the knife, confused. "What?"

"I didn't think so. I can kill you right now, you know. Run this through you here." He slid the knife down his rib cage, and Ethan held the point over his heart.

"I don't know you."

Ethan snorted. "Lies." He pushed on the blade just enough to make it a threat. "No one would blame me if I killed you. Wolf, hunter. We obviously hate each other, don't we? Shame I can't remember if things were ever any different."

The blade pierced his skin just enough to bring a drop of blood. Liam arched his back, struggled with strength he didn't have against the cuffs.

"I guess you have to trust that I am a better man than that." Of course he was. His lie was falling apart with each breath. He was not Fiona. He was not Charles. He was a good man. But he couldn't just stop now.

Liam coughed dryly. "I know of you. I mean, who doesn't, right? But I don't know you. That night in the forest… I'd only just got here. I lived here when I was a kid and left a long time ago. I haven't been back until now." It took him a while to get out the words. There was a hint of terror swirling beneath the bravado, and Ethan saw a little crack in Liam that mirrored his own.

"Okay, and I suppose, then, that you have a reasonable explanation for my sister's reaction to you, if you haven't been around to piss her off?" He wouldn't go into detail about his memory loss. Something told him revealing too much would hinder a confession even more.

Liam breathed in. "Never seen her before. Maybe I look like someone else? I—"

But the blade found its way back to Liam's stomach, trailing blood as it went, and Ethan and Liam both watched it again with morbid fascination as the red swirled with the motion of the knife.

He dipped it down low, just below the low-slung waistband of Liam's sweats, wanting so much for the action to be a threat and not a discovery, but Liam's hips jerked, and if Ethan hadn't seen his erection beneath the fabric before, there was no way he missed it now.

Ethan's mouth opened as he tore his gaze away from the slowing trickle of blood. He took a breath and swiped the knife over the fabric, and his heart stopped when Liam's cock twitched.

"Is this...?" He shook his head. "You like this."

It was not a question. He already knew the answer. Probably the only answer he was going to get tonight anyway.

The knife rested on Liam's cock, only a layer of cotton separated the two. He arched up into it, as if seeking the friction. Ethan's mouth hung open. His chest rose and fell rapidly.

What the hell am I doing?

His hand moved to just above Liam's cock. He could feel the warmth of it, and Liam jerked into it, giving everything away.

Liam's eyes were dark, and he was not looking away from Ethan.

"Keep going." It was barely a whisper, probably all he could manage in this state, but it was not a request to be ignored.

Ethan's hand wrapped around him tentatively, but even the light touch was enough to make Liam whimper. Ethan bit his lip, never broke eye contact with Liam, and—as if his verbal consent hadn't been enough—only moved again when Liam thrust up into his fist, baring his teeth, almost growling his demand for him to do *something*.

"Don't stop. Ethan, please."

But the words brought him back instead of sending him over the edge. *This isn't you, Ethan. This isn't you at all. What would your wife say?*

Ethan pulled back. Liam groaned in frustration at the sudden loss of contact.

"Not like this. This isn't—I don't want to hurt you, Liam. Not like this."

Liam smiled lazily and blinked, refocusing in an instant. Ethan couldn't help but recall those same words from Liam not a day before.

"Yes, you do, Ethan." *Come get me.* The tables had turned completely.

"I'm still.... You're not going to get me to stop...." Ethan could barely get the words out.

"Oh, Ethan. Neither of us is stupid enough to think that you're not still going to run that knife clean through me. This isn't my first experience with the wrong end of a Robertson weapon, if you recall. This time is much more pleasant, though."

Liam squeezed his thighs, pulled on the cuffs, eyes wide open as if to take in every reaction Ethan had to watching him. Ethan knew his pupils were blown, and this wasn't curiosity or experimentation or some sick, sadistic game. They were both getting off on this. Ethan wouldn't have been surprised if he came in his jeans from just watching, rutting against Liam while he thrust up into Ethan and, goddamn, if Liam were just strong enough, he would have thrown him down on the mattress for a bit of payback for looking like that while Ethan was trying so hard to just stab the bastard already.

But the thought of throwing Liam down and fucking him, of Ethan stripping all the way and easing himself onto Liam, riding him, coming on top of him, breaking that intense stare to close his eyes and come screaming his name, it was intoxicating, too much to stay focused.

Ethan felt the moment he broke, the moment when an already bad idea, fueled by his dreams, his obsessive needs, became even worse. He felt the moment he stopped caring about anything but what was happening right then. The moment he forgot to care about the consequences.

Ethan's hand was dry save for the sweat of trepidation, of arousal, and he was not so far gone that he didn't notice it, thankfully. The little jar of salve was still by the bedside, and it was not long before the dry slide of flesh on flesh became slippery, if sweet-smelling. It was slow, cautious, like he was deciding every stroke was one step closer to damnation, but he didn't stop either.

"Good?" Like he didn't know. Like he couldn't see Liam's toes curl and his hips arch.

"Yeah. Yeah. It's good."

The confirmation emboldened Ethan even more. The bed squeaked as he joined Liam on it, straddling his thighs and bringing his own erection grinding down on Liam. He slipped his own shirt over his head, and it was cruel torture that Liam couldn't touch him back like this.

Liam was getting close. He was getting close, and neither of them knew what this whole spectacle was actually supposed to accomplish. He could lie all he wanted to, to Liam, to himself, about healing spells and poison and research, but they both knew this was something darker and more intriguing. Like they had something to prove to each other but they couldn't quite say what.

He couldn't last, not like that. Ethan sped up, tightened his grip, and it was what he needed.

"That's it, Liam. Come for me. Let me hear it. Let me see it." Every muscle in Liam's body tensed, and he couldn't control his breathing or the noises that came out of his mouth. He was coming hard, and Ethan leaned forward, trapped his spasming dick between them, and kissed him roughly, biting at his lips and swallowing his cries. The skin-on-skin intensified every sensation, and it was only when he could breathe again, when Ethan's heart stopped banging in his ears like gunshots, that he slid the blade between Liam's ribs, the stretch and pull of pierced flesh, the warm gush of blood spilling down his side to pool at his back. Only then could he manage to whisper, "I'm sorry. I'm sorry. I'm sorry." Until Liam passed out once again.

It was some time after Ethan performed the healing spell, cleaned up Liam, and moved him to the more comfortable guest room that he began to relive what had just happened over and over in his mind.

Over the line and against every rule. Why would he do that? With a wolf? An enemy? These dreams were fucking with him when he was awake now too. It was the only explanation. He had to find a way to stop them before he did something really stupid.

Despite his stupidity, though, *the spell had worked,* but was this really the best way to find a new way to kill their kind? He played it again in his head, and he should have been getting off on the sensation of the knife sliding in, scraping against bone and tearing through muscle. That was what should get him hard, not the look on Liam's face when he came, the noises he made, the lingering taste of him on Ethan's lips....

He waited in his bedroom until he heard Liam puttering around in the hallway. The light was on in the bathroom, and Ethan knocked on the door.

"I have a shirt for you. Shoes too. You're free to go, Liam."

Liam opened the door, and Ethan refused to look him in the eye.

"Here. They should fit."

"Ethan—"

"The spell worked. You held up your end of the bargain." He would not lift his gaze. The guilt radiated from him. "Please, Liam." He shoved the clothing into Liam's arms.

"Ethan." Liam dropped the shirt and shoes on the floor and pulled Ethan inside the bathroom, pulled him close, and slammed the door. Liam shoved him up against it.

Ethan was certainly looking at Liam now. Ethan reached up to push him away. "Liam, I...."

Liam captured his hands and pinned them above his head.

"It's not... I can't...."

Liam leaned in and scented his neck. "God...." He inhaled again. Ethan swore he heard him mumble something about fire under his breath. "You know what you did to me. I know you wanted it too. You're just as twisted as you think I am."

Liam kissed him in a harsh, broken rhythm, but instead of anger, all Ethan could feel was that it wasn't enough. That nothing would ever be enough when it came to Liam. They were not kids. He needed more and he was going to take it from Liam, angrily grasping his jaw and yanking him up to his own mouth, and Liam took the hint and kissed him back, rough and hot and *needy*. Liam's hand snaked down to palm Ethan's crotch, and something snapped in Ethan. He finally found the means to push Liam off.

"I wanted this? I'm a married man, Liam. Married to a *human*. Why would I...?"

Liam let out a snort of derision. "Like this is your first tussle with one of my kind. Please. Sell me another lie, Ethan. I can hear your heartbeat. You can't lie to me. Can't hide the bulge in your jeans, the smell of you right now. It's driving me *insane*. You like being the prey for once. Tell me, how many times have you fantasized about this? How many times have you had my name on your lips and come on your fingers?"

"I don't.... You know what? I think it's time you go." Ethan struggled against Liam's grip.

"Yeah, you got what you wanted, didn't you? A new way to kill me. To kill my people." Liam finally let him go with a disgusted look on his face, although Ethan couldn't tell if it was disgust for him or for Liam himself.

Ethan shook his head because it wasn't like that at all.

"And here I thought...." Liam backed away with something that looked a lot like hurt in his eyes. He pursed his lips together and nodded. "Yeah. You're right. I'm going to go. Good-bye, Ethan. It's been... memorable."

Ethan didn't move from the wall until he heard the front door click.

He tossed the cot that night and burned every bandage, every towel, every shred of evidence that Liam Kinnaird was ever in his home, his mind... and certainly not ever in his mouth, his hand, coating his skin with come and blood.

The next night, when Moira came home, he fucked her roughly on the floor, didn't even let her get all the way undressed before he threw her down and shoved into her. She loved it, didn't understand that it was convenience and frustration driving him. It had been months since they last had sex, but he didn't notice her squeals or when she came—twice—because all he could see behind his tightly shut eyes, all he could hear, all he could feel, was Liam.

CHAPTER 18

TWO NIGHTS later, his phone chirped.

It was Fiona.

The pack has attacked again.

It was time for everyone to fight.

Ethan gathered his weapons and caught up with everyone outside Fiona's before heading out with them to chase down the pack on the other side of town.

And it came as no surprise that Liam had joined the pack. He must have stayed after Ethan brought him here. He must have caught wind of the pack in town.

Liam had claimed Ethan for his own and he delivered blow after blow, probably some payback for what happened—and what hadn't happened—the last time they'd crossed paths, and the blows became harder when Ethan tried to attack another wolf.

Liam leaned in close. "I don't think so, Ethan. Why start another fight when you can't even finish this one?"

Another body blow. He felt a rib crack from the impact and maybe another one go as he bounced off the concrete when he fell. Liam's eyes flashed as he went down to straddle Ethan, kneeing him in the stomach as he did. Ethan tried to suppress the pathetic whimper as much from the pain as it was from the insane sense memory he had developed from his vivid dreams.

"Don't know when to quit, do you, Ethan? You *never* know when to quit! You *never* learn, do you?" Liam growled just a few inches from his face.

"Then teach me." The words tumbled out and it was too late to take them back. *You never learn. When will you ever learn?* How many times had he dreamed that? *Won't you ever learn that I care for you more than that psycho ever could?* Why did that sound so familiar? Being on the ground with Liam above and fighting all around them. Did that happen before?

Ethan tasted the blood in his mouth and spat it out in time to see a fist fly toward his face.

Liam paused midblow and breathed in sharply, eyebrows knitting together in something that looked like confusion to Ethan. "You *never....*" Liam breathed in again and again, like he could scent something in the air. Something changed in Liam's face, his eyes, for just a split second.

"What, *wolf,* can't finish what you started?" Breathing had started to hurt now, but he couldn't look away from Liam's blue eyes, softened then and very confused, looking off in the distance, like there was something just on the edge of his memory that he couldn't see all of. He mumbled under his breath again, this time something about being the only way.

"Liam, do it. It's the only way."

"Liam. I'm ready. I can take it. Do it."

The words floated through Ethan's head, and the line between what was real and what he had been dreaming about was as blurry as his vision.

Liam shook his head like he had come out of a fog.

Ethan felt a sharp crack across his face, and everything went dark.

He drifted in and out of consciousness for a bit, hearing voices saying things he couldn't hope to interpret through the haze. He struggled to focus on the nagging feeling that there was something *very strange* going on, but the pain overtook him as someone shoved a hand up underneath his spine to lift him and he passed out cold.

HE AWOKE sometime later, sore and alone, shirtless. And in a strange bed. His injuries had been wrapped and compressed neatly. He didn't remember how he got there or who got him there, but he was not dead, so there must have been at least a small victory on their side. *Someone* had to live to get him here. There was no way he did this on his own.

He noted, with some small relief, that at least this sleep had been a dreamless one, but that thought was soon overtaken with the memory of Liam's face before he had passed out.

He replayed the moment over and over in his mind, each time zeroing in on Liam's reaction and the weird flash of what felt like a memory right before everything went black. For the first time, he let the inevitable conclusion wash over him, form the words in his brain he couldn't yet say aloud, that maybe—no, more than maybe—these weren't just dreams.

But certainly he would remember being on such... good terms with someone, right? His history with that family was nothing anyone could ever say anything good about. It was Fiona who dealt the most with them before the accident.

And Liam reacting the way he did, well, that just added another layer to the mystery.

Ethan gingerly rolled onto his side and fumbled in the dark to see if his phone was within reach. His phone and maybe a note or some other clue as to how he'd got here. He got lucky with the former and struck out on the latter, but there were at least twenty texts from Fiona, from Moira, from his kids, demanding to know where he was and why he had left.

Well, he could rule them out. He texted them back, not giving away too much, just that he needed to tend to his injuries and they were pretty bad.

He breathed in sharply and tried to sit up. He found some more small relief when he could do so easier than he thought he could. Whoever had treated him knew what he or she was doing.

His phone chirped, and it was Fiona, naturally, demanding he regroup with everyone else, like, yesterday. *Injuries be damned* went unsaid. Obviously, in her mind, the ability to text back meant he wasn't dead or otherwise busy dying.

Ethan rolled his eyes and threw his phone down on the bed so he could concentrate on standing. It took three minutes, but once he was upright, he was pretty sure he could stay that way. He wasn't going to get any points for his fashion sense or for the way his shirt hung over the layers of bandages and compression wraps, but as long as he was counting small victories, he managed to be able to use both arms to dress himself, so there were no broken bones there.

He opened the curtains a little to get his bearings and saw the bright red of a neon motel sign. It was on the other side of town from where he had been, too far to walk even when he was not nursing a broken rib, but before he thought to call and ask for a ride, he spied his truck parked in the tiny lot below. A search of the room turned up his keys. Someone had gone through a lot of trouble to see him safe.

He let his sister know he was on his way, forcing himself to forget, if even for a little bit, about Liam.

WALLY'S WAS a small bar on the southern end of town and also the designated meet point to regroup. The owner was a trusted ally and kept a room in the back for times like these, when it was too dangerous for any one hunter to be caught alone.

Fiona was pacing back and forth when Ethan walked in. She didn't stop to acknowledge Ethan as he limped to a chair in the back of the dimly lit room, dodging panicked questions from Moira and the kids when the extent of his injuries became obvious.

There was no plan, no real recourse or idea what to do next.

Ethan knew Fiona needed everyone present and accounted for before she could even start to plan the next move. Pack mentality. Ironic. Even the mere hint of it turned his stomach.

Fiona still wasn't acting like a leader. She stopped occasionally to survey the action in the room, but nothing ever changed. She was acting like a paranoid killer.

And all this silence wasn't helping Ethan stay distracted long. It had become awkward, too awkward, and Ethan felt no obligation to stay while Fiona paced and muttered while she thought.

He stood to leave, but Fiona was on him in a heartbeat. "Going somewhere, Ethan?"

Injured and annoyed, now was not the time to start a fight. "Yeah, Fiona, sitting here in silence isn't getting anything done." But Ethan had never really respected too many boundaries like that.

His sister's eyes threatened to roll out of her head. "And what are *you* gonna do, Ethan? Run away some more?" *Weak. Injured. Breakable. Useless.* He could see the words float in the air around him. "You left in the middle of the fight, and you're leaving now. What are you going to do when you go out there all alone and you can't run? I knew bringing you back after the explosion was a bad idea. I have too much to worry about already without—"

"In the middle of the— Jesus, Fiona. You throw my weakness in my face constantly and then act all surprised when I fall because of it. In case you didn't know, I went down fighting. Yeah, I'm not at my peak. Are you going to leave me for dead because I'm just not worth it anymore? I swear, the older you get, the less human you become. You're becoming one of *them*, Fiona."

The room had gone silent. It was almost amusing that Fiona could not command this kind of attention any other way.

Fiona smiled and nodded her head. "You're one to talk, brother."

Ethan froze. "What is that supposed to mean, exactly?"

"It means—" Fiona pursed her lips together. "It means you're done here. You need to go. *Now.*"

"What are you playing at?" Ethan didn't go for the door. Fiona was unhinged and had a secret, and this may have been his best chance to get it out of her. He marched right to her, got in her face, and dared her to do something about it.

She stared at him for what felt like an hour before speaking, and when she did, it was low and threatening. "You'll be wanting to get away from me right now, Ethan. Just turn around and walk out the door."

He moved closer to her. He could feel her breath on his face. He was not going to let her win. *"Or what?"*

Her mouth twisted into a sick grin. "Oh, brother. Don't try me. What I'm playing at could ruin your life." She breathed and grabbed him by his shoulders to whisper in his ear. "I've been keeping your secrets for twenty-three years because you're family. You're all I have left. And you can be a damned good hunter. But right now? You're *useless*. And I don't protect the useless. I could take away your happy little lie of a life in a snap. Your marriage, your children, the protection being with other hunters affords you—I can make it all go away with the dirt I have on you. And I'm sure everyone here, including Moira and my darling niece and nephew, would love to hear what I can spill. So, do yourself and your wife and children a favor, and *just leave*."

She let him go and waited for him to make his move with a sickly sweet smile on her face. He looked to Moira and Jamie and Katie. They were watching him expectantly, as was everyone else in the room. He took a deep breath and made his decision.

Ethan slammed the door behind him and walked to his truck.

Unfortunately, his plan to wait for Fiona to be alone and get to the bottom of this had to take a backseat to the swift and generous ingestion of painkillers. Only part of him didn't hope the chemicals in them would force his subconscious to reveal some more of its secrets.

He slept in his truck that night along the edge of the forest, ignoring Moira's phone calls and not even caring that the drugs would render him unable to defend himself if something—someone—came along.

Liam woke him from a dead sleep, naked and sliding a warm hand down his chest, and he smiled sleepily in the darkness.

"Can't sleep?" Ethan stretched a little, arched into his touch, warm, familiar, comforting, and he propped himself up on his elbow.

Liam didn't say anything as he pushed the silky sheet down a little, giving himself more skin to touch and explore, fingers curling into the soft hair on Ethan's bare chest. He reached up and caressed his cheek, pulled Ethan down for a kiss, and didn't care that he hadn't brushed his teeth. The need he felt overtook any petty concern over early morning breath.

Liam's hand worked its way lower, sliding over the muscles of Ethan's belly until he found his erection straining against his boxers. Liam cupped it, long fingers wrapping around him through the fabric, and Ethan hissed a bit against his lips. Liam responded with a playful nip to his lower lip, and after all this time, he still couldn't believe his luck getting to be with this sexy, formidable creature.

Liam wanted those boxers off, and Ethan wouldn't dare deny him the unspoken request. He lifted up his hips and he sat up more to strip them away, and he didn't notice or care where they went.

Ethan ran his hands along Liam's side, feeling hard bumps of muscle and smooth skin, but his gentle attempts to guide him on top didn't follow Liam's plan, and it was abundantly clear just who was in charge when he moved down and settled himself between Ethan's legs.

He took Ethan between his lips, all luscious wetness and heat, knowing instinctively at this point in their marriage just how he wanted it, swirling his tongue around him and hollowing his cheeks, taking his time to make sure Ethan lasted.

He could feel Liam's hips jerk every time he let out a moan, knowing every noise he made got Liam harder, and when Ethan reached down to run his fingers through his hair, Liam squeezed Ethan's hip with his free hand.

Liam knew—of course he knew—before he went too far, and he pulled away, quickly straddling Ethan before he could protest the loss of contact too much.

Ethan reached up and splayed his hand over Liam's chest and ran his thumbs over his hard nipples. Ethan delighted in the small noises and sighs Liam made.

Liam rubbed himself against Ethan's erection, and he must have planned it because he was so prepared for him already. It would have been so easy to slip inside Liam, make him cry out for Ethan as he thrust up into him, and as much as he loved Liam's bossy streak in bed, he was not going to be able to wait much longer before he took control and fucked him.

Liam must have sensed his impatience, though, and how much he had already driven Ethan out of his mind, and gave him the teasing promise of relief, lifting up his hips to let Ethan reach between them to guide himself to Liam's entrance. He shivered on top of Ethan as he lowered himself slowly, torturously, letting him feel just how wet and how tight he truly was, centimeter by centimeter.

"Baby, please...."

Liam grasped Ethan's hips and he rocked them against him, lowering himself all the way, and he sighed contentedly. It was only then that he leaned in and kissed Ethan again, continuing the slow rhythm with his hips. He could just make out Liam's face in the moonlight: his eyes were closed in absolute bliss, lips swollen and parted. He was exquisite, divine, and all Ethan's.

He knew Liam was close. Knew from the gorgeous noises he made: his name, choked, bitten off, litanies of "oh, God," and low, breathy moans. Knew from the delicious tightening he felt around him, how much tighter he got as he moved. Liam buried his head into the crook of Ethan's neck, biting the sensitive flesh there, and Ethan held him close as he shuddered against him, picking up the rhythm where he failed, and he was sweating against him and crying out and it was still the most beautiful thing he had ever seen after all this time.

"I love you, Liam." He whispered it against his cheek.

Ethan thrust through his aftershocks, gently, so Liam would know he would let him take over when he was ready again. It didn't take long, though, for Liam to find the rhythm again, and he sped up, going as deeply as he could, and Ethan was not going to take long no matter how hard he tried to hold out.

He sat up again, letting Liam caress his skin as much as he wanted, and Ethan threw his head back, completely lost in feeling.

Ethan returned his hands to Liam's hips, setting the speed for him, but something was wrong. Something was different. Ethan's hands were wet, warm, and he brought them to his face to try to see what was on them. His hands were black in the darkness and it could have meant only one thing. Blood.

He tried to sit up, tried to see in the darkness, to protect Liam, but he found himself paralyzed from the belly up. He looked up at Liam. Blood poured from a hole that seemed to go right through him, but he hadn't stopped riding Ethan either. Ethan strained to see, to open his mouth to yell, but Liam seemed oblivious to his injury.

He pushed, struggled to move, but Liam continued his pace, and all Ethan could do was watch in a terrifying panic.

"Mmmm... how could you forget this? How could you forget us, Ethan?"

A loud bang echoed throughout him and he was suddenly in a dark warehouse. Liam was crying and so was he.

Fiona, fifteen and cocky, strutted toward them.

"Yeah, Ethan. How could you forget this? Or, more to the point, how could you forget her?"

Moira came out of the shadows and she, too, was crying. She held a crossbow at Ethan's heart to keep him in place.

"Weren't you happy? Look at everyone now. Everything was perfect before you came along, Liam." Fiona walked to Liam and cupped his jaw roughly. She whispered something into his ear that Ethan couldn't hear. The white noise of anger and panic drowned out everything.

Liam didn't respond but Fiona still giggled. Something silver flashed in the moonlight. Fiona ran a sgian-dubh *through Liam's heart. Liam froze in panic, and Ethan could only watch in horror as the light left Liam's eyes, as he slid to the ground in a heap.*

Fiona laughed and pulled the blade from Liam's chest, wiping the blood off on her skirt. She turned to Moira and gently forced her to lower the crossbow.

"It's okay, Moira. You've done nothing wrong to deserve this blood on your hands. Let me."

Fiona placed the blade against Ethan's chest.

"You're next, Ethan. And then?" She shrugged and batted her eyelashes. "I'm coming for Katie. And Jamie. And everyone you love until I've righted the dishonor you brought on the family."

Ethan tried to fight, to kick, to push up, yell, anything, but Fiona tangled herself up with Ethan, any small movements he could make swallowed up by Fiona's strength. She wrapped her hands around his neck, choking him, squeezing the breath out of him, and still Fiona laughed. He gasped for breath, and just as he regained a tiny bit of control over his limbs....

He woke up. Alone. Wrestling with the jacket he'd thrown over himself as a makeshift blanket. He was soaked in sweat, and tears stung his eyes. He threw open the truck door and retched on the loamy earth outside.

It was cold out, probably, but he felt nothing on the outside to match the numbness on the inside.

But every scratch, every twig snap, started to bring him to a focused alertness he hadn't felt in a long time.

It may not have been a memory, but he felt like the nightmare gave him some insight where he had only had vague flashes of thought about before. He knew, he was more sure than ever, that Fiona didn't just know what had happened to him, what was happening to him now. Fiona may have played a role in making it happen.

He had to rest. Had to sleep off the meds in his system so he could think clearly about his next move. There was no point running off to accuse her without some kind of proof beyond a painkiller-induced nightmare that felt like the truth. And he still couldn't even prove he and Liam had ever been together. How could he even prove such a thing when….

A sudden realization hit him. It was a thought, a feeling, a memory, something snapped his brain to attention and he knew what he had to do.

CHAPTER 19

ETHAN WAS still a bit blinded by the bright morning sun. It was 9:00 a.m. He was, predictably, more sore than he had been yesterday, but that persistent undercurrent in the back of his mind forced him to risk the fight and frustration to go home.

He drove up to a thankfully empty house. He had a feeling Fiona had forced everyone to go about their daily business to keep up the lie that they were just a normal family.

Something compelled him to the attic, into boxes he hadn't seen the inside of for years. He didn't know what he was looking for, but he knew he would know when he saw it. He went through boxes of Jamie's baby things, of Katie's, of wedding photos. What he needed went back farther.

Three hours and what seemed like a thousand boxes later, he trudged downstairs with a photo album in hand.

It was labeled "Summer 1990," and it was filled with college girls in flannel and jean shorts over tights with crunchy, gravity-defying bangs, and guys with ripped jeans, Doc Martens, and long, unkempt hair. If his life depended on naming one person in there, he would be dead by the first page.

He flipped through, not exactly knowing why. Just a niggling feeling in that dark recess of his mind, the one protected by a high wall that seemed to be showing some cracks lately.

It was on the third to last page that he found exactly what he didn't know he was looking for.

Behind a bland picture of him and some random people posed in front of an ice cream stand somewhere on a Gulf Coast beach was another picture.

He held his breath and slipped it from the plastic cover.

The people in the picture were on the ground. The warm yellow sunlight illuminated the summer wildflowers around them. One person was looking up at the camera: A young, smiling Ethan, lighter blond and skinnier.

And the other, a dark-haired, blue-eyed boy who was instead gazing at Ethan with a look of such intense affection it made Ethan's jaw drop.

Liam.

THE REST of the day was a blur. Or, rather, a Liam-shaped blur. Ethan could barely manage to tear his eyes from the photograph, searching every centimeter of it for clues as to how this could have happened and he not remember it. Everything he had been dreaming had really happened. He knew that with alarming certainty. How could he have forgotten?

Liam.

Ethan and Liam. Young, crazy, just like in his dreams... obviously not dreams now. No sane person could deny that. Not when there was a very real possibility that he might actually have been in love with Liam. The feelings he felt when he dreamed—even in his head, they were stronger than what he had ever felt for Moira. His brain couldn't fully remember, but his heart ached every time he saw Liam, even the one in his dreams. How could he have forgotten being in love with him?

He couldn't eat, couldn't move from the dining room table, not for hours. He turned himself inside out trying to remember more. And he knew that if he could just chip away at the dark wall in his mind holding that time hostage, he would know how he came to forget in the first place.

And in that same vein, he wondered if Liam knew. If he knew and had been keeping it from him all this time. Or had he forgotten too?

No, that look on his face, the haunted chaos that flashed in his eyes for a split second—he knew something.

And it may not have been his finest plan ever—none ever were—but he stupidly placed the truth above his life for the moment and went to look for Liam to find out what he knew. Past or not, Ethan did not like it one bit that there was part of his life missing, and if Liam had something to do with it too, then God help him.

But if Liam was a difficult man to find with a group of hunters, then he was damned near impossible for just one man to locate.

He searched for hours—every dark, dank warehouse, abandoned storefront, even the deepest recesses of the forests, and came up empty-handed. He found and questioned, with probably more force than necessary, a few half-breeds with wavering loyalty—the right answer for the right price—but they knew nothing more than he did. One swore he had seen some of the pack tear through a back alley just hours before, but there was no one who looked over twenty-five. No one had anything useful.

Ethan was sore and frustrated, and it was nearing midnight. He should have been falling into bed with something powerful washed down with whiskey, but he was wide-awake. He wouldn't stop until he had answers.

He stayed out all night, driving, wandering, hoping to catch a glimpse of Liam, in some form, somewhere in the dark. He drove south toward home, thinking he had run back to where Ethan had found him that day, bleeding and dying, but as the sun rose, he didn't hold out much hope anymore.

Sometime around 8:00 a.m., he found himself driving out of town, heading northeast up and across old familiar highways. Before he knew it, before he realized what he had done, he was just outside of Cocoa, climbing out of his truck and walking toward that familiar spot like it was something he did every day instead of something he hadn't done for years and had completely forgotten ever doing.

Every tree, every bush, every rock was simultaneously a discovery and a jog in his memory. He didn't know where he was going, but he trusted his subconscious to get him to where some answers might be.

He touched sun-warmed bark, and instantly a memory of Liam laughing, grabbing at his hand to pull him along faster, his fingers catching on every tree in mock protest as he dragged him, flashed in front of his eyes.

He spied an old downed tree to the side, and he could see Liam pinning him up against it, using it for leverage as they rutted against it, Liam whispering the dirtiest sweet nothings in his ear, grinning wolfishly when Ethan faltered from just thinking about what Liam had suggested.

He walked—well, limped—for ten minutes… twenty… a rumbling sense of purpose growing steadily inside him, thrumming in his ears over the din of nature and his footsteps in the underbrush.

The clearing was just up ahead. He knew without seeing it. Their clearing. Their special place where no one else could find them. Some answers were here, he swore. Something here would tell him what he wanted to know.

What he didn't expect to find in that clearing, though, was Liam, half-transformed, ready to fight, claws extended and growling as he stared right at Ethan.

"How the hell did you find me, Robertson?"

He didn't wait for an answer. Before Ethan could open his mouth to respond, Liam knocked him to the ground and pounced on top of him. Ethan yelped as a fresh burst of pain radiated from his rib cage. Liam raised his hand and fully extended a single claw, tracing it along Ethan's skin until it reached his carotid artery. One slice and he would be bleeding out, dead in minutes.

He closed his eyes, breathed in sharply, and hoped there was something in Liam, something, some remnant of feeling or memory that, like in Ethan, was bursting to escape his brain. Something that would remind him he hadn't always wanted to kill Ethan.

"Please, Liam. We need to talk." He arched his head back, exposing more neck to Liam, a show of submission.

Liam growled, seemed to have laser sight focused on him. The wolf was taking control now. He leaned in close to Ethan's neck, inhaling deeply, and Ethan knew he could smell fear on others. Fear and lies and danger.

He was not lying. He was unarmed. And he was terrified.

But Liam wasn't stopping. He held himself there under Ethan's jaw and breathed him in for a few more seconds. Ethan couldn't stand much more. Liam, the real Liam, being this close to him, warm breath on his skin, and dreams or not, he couldn't deny the feeling coupled with the very real danger he was in was getting him just a little hard.

When he finally pulled away, Liam was no longer the half-transformed wolf. In fact, he looked utterly... human. Lost, confused, with tears in his eyes that just seemed to confuse him more. He quickly scrambled off Ethan and retreated away from him.

"What have you done to me, Ethan? How are you doing this? I see you every time I close my eyes. Have been since I... since I came back. I see you in my dreams and they're so... real. Always the same thing too. We're...." He shook his head like he wanted to clear the images from his brain.

"And then you act like you can see inside my head. I know you're behind it all. I just don't know how. Is this one of your *hunter* tricks? How does harassing me like this stick to your 'laws'?"

Ethan opened his mouth to speak, but Liam wasn't finished.

"And then, after all that, you come and find me *here*? I found this place when I was a kid, and I never told anyone about it, and you just waltz in here like you have a map to it seared into your brain. So, obviously you're in my head, making me see things and question my own sanity.

"Well, I'll tell you, Ethan, I don't have much sanity left to take, so just undo whatever Jedi mind trick you've done to me and let's kill each other the normal way, okay? Honestly, though, I have to admire your imagination. The things you've made me see, what you made me do... I didn't think you had it in you."

"Liam, I—" Liam thought Ethan was doing this to him on purpose.

"No. You know something? I don't even care how you did it. Just... stop. I should have killed you that night. Hell, how many chances have I had to kill you? I should have ripped you open without a care in the world, or worse, turned you. But I couldn't. Because you've effectively neutered me up here." He pointed to his head with two fingers, like he wished they were a gun.

"Liam, if you'd just let me—"

Liam's eyes flashed and anger replaced the confusion on his face in a heartbeat. He flew at Ethan again, rough and desperate.

"No one should have this kind of power over me! I *protected* you the other night! Why would I do that? I picked you up and took you away from the fight, and before I knew it, I was *fixing* you. *Helping* you. And the whole time I couldn't shake the feeling that there was something so familiar about it. I have to give you credit for this. It's genius, fucking with me like this. Even now, I could tear you apart and no one would ever know, and all I want to do is—"

Liam stopped abruptly, obviously having realized every word had brought him closer to Ethan's lips. He was so close Ethan could feel the heat radiate from him, and he was not making the effort to move away.

Ethan stayed silent, didn't break eye contact with Liam. He knew Liam could hear his heart pounding, and he didn't know how Liam would interpret that in his manic, paranoid state. He was completely exposed and vulnerable, and for the first time since he'd got there, he damned himself for not bringing a weapon.

And then there was the matter of his erection, which hadn't subsided in the least.

Liam growled in frustration. Or in resignation. Ethan couldn't tell until Liam closed the gap between them and kissed him violently, pushing past his lips and into his mouth like he needed it to survive. He wound his hands down to find Ethan's and yanked them up over his head, pinning them there painfully with one hand.

Ethan whimpered into his mouth, jerking his hips up because he didn't know what else he should do. It was wrong, wrong, wrong like this, but it was so much better than his dreams, so much more right than what had happened in the garage. Liam's hot mouth on his, body heavy on top of him, grinding into him hard so there was no way he couldn't feel his cock through his jeans, and Liam was probably not even aware that he was doing it, avoiding putting too much pressure on Ethan's hurt rib.

Liam squeezed his wrists together so Ethan could feel the bones rub against each other. He was distantly worried they might break under his grip, but Liam made a noise that distracted him from that thought. Ethan hissed and lifted his chin again, and this time Liam wasn't satisfied just scenting him. He nipped at the skin there with sharp teeth that threatened to break the skin, and Ethan forced himself not to tense up. The show of bravery—or stupidity—seemed to turn Liam on even more.

He used his free hand to reach between them, to palm Ethan's cock through his jeans. Ethan's head fell back and he arched into it, pushing more of him into Liam to let him know that, yes, he wanted more than anything for this to actually happen. He would never be able to pinpoint the second that became a possibility in his mind, but the little voice inside him that would usually question that desire had been strangely quiet lately.

"Please, Liam! Please!" And as soon as the words tumbled out, he regretted them.

Liam stopped just as quickly as he had started. The spell was broken.

"Fuck, Robertson! You think this is funny?" Liam looked horrified. "Don't do this to me again! Or the next time I see you—in reality or in my dreams—I *will* kill you. I don't care how you try to stop me. And don't ever let me catch you here again."

Liam leaped off Ethan and disappeared before he could protest, leaving Ethan alone in the clearing.

It was not exactly the answer he had been hoping for as a million new questions formed in his mind.

CHAPTER 20

ETHAN DIDN'T see Liam for weeks. He didn't exactly search for him, though, not knowing what to say to him after their last encounter, and Liam was definitely no longer running with his new pack, so the opportunities to see him weren't exactly numerous.

He barely spoke to Moira those days. He had to process everything. He was not sure how he felt about anything or anyone now, and as much as it was not fair to put her out, even though she had nothing to do with this, it was equally not fair that all this new information made him question if he had ever really loved her at all, if love was what he felt when he was asleep. Moira was... convenient. It was some time after the explosion that he met her. She was pretty, yeah, but competent and smart as a whip. She filled a hole in his life that he didn't know he had until she kissed him for the first time.

He married her soon after she had graduated from college. For love? Maybe. No, not love. Respect. Mutual respect and fondness and common interests. Fiona always called them a "smart match."

He'd never had any real plans to get back into hunting after the accident. He had the perfect excuse not to, but it was Moira who gave him the push. She was as interested in Ethan's hunting past as Ethan was in leaving it behind, but parts of the old him bled through, and simple field archery lessons turned to semiautomatic lessons and soon, too soon, she was eager to try out her skills. *There's no harm in teaching her to protect herself,* he told himself. *Man or monster, she needs to defend herself if ever I can't.*

It wasn't long before she caught wind of dead bodies in the forests from Fiona. They were mutilated. Bitten. Ethan spent a long, restless night in his favorite chair beating himself up for even entertaining the thought of going back to that life and bringing his wife, the mother of his child, into it too.

In the end, they hunted. They started small. Dead bodies showed up, and they investigated and contained the threat. More dead bodies, mutilations, hints of magic, they were right there taking care of it.

And if he stopped to think about it, he really enjoyed it—hunting, hunting for the *right* reasons and not Fiona's crazy vendetta, was satisfying, if dirty, work.

And working with his wife was a whole new level of commitment, of trust, of intimacy in their marriage. She took to hunting like a fish to water, and her strict adherence to the commitment to only contain threats made her an ideal partner in work and in other areas of their life together. It made the sex better, sure. The adrenaline of a successful hunt filled in the gaps where his passion just wasn't. It was not her fault he needed the rush to bring himself to where he should naturally be. Moira was beautiful and sexy and willing and formidable and everything he should want in that area.

Should.

And now he knew why she wasn't.

THE SOLITUDE gave him time to think, to research, to try to pin down exactly how they could have both lost their memory like that. Pinpoint, laser-etched memory loss wasn't something he came across every day. Dark magic came up frequently. He hadn't wanted to give too many details to Tim. Maybe to keep him safe if Fiona caught wind. Maybe due to embarrassment of not being able to remember so much of his life that apparently mattered a lot. Maybe he just wasn't willing to admit to anyone yet that he'd broken an important rule by taking up with a werewolf, with a Kinnaird. Tim was good and didn't ask many questions beyond the scope of the memory loss. He came back empty-handed, saying if it was magic, it sounded old, maybe ancient, and could probably only be performed by someone with an expert knowledge of the practice.

It should have been a relief to hear that. Fiona was a lot of things, but an expert in magic, something that required a subtlety and calm Fiona did not possess, was not one of them.

That meant there might be more than one person involved. More mysteries to solve. Just what he needed.

He also took time to meditate to try to force himself to remember more, like how he and Liam had met, how they came to start a relationship, their first kiss, did they fight, did they break up....

"Mom thinks you're cheating on her." Katie sauntered into his office and plopped down in a chair.

"What? Did Mom tell you that?" He was not ready for this. Saying it out loud made it real.

"Not me, no." She shrugged her shoulders and took out her phone.

"Katie." He pinched the bridge of his nose.

"Okay, I sort of heard her talking to Aunt Fi." Her ability to talk seriously and still text a million messages a minute was not the sort of ability the noble Robertsons of the past had hoped for the future generations of warriors.

"*Katie*, we've talked about this a thousand—wait, what did Aunt Fi say?"

"'Moira, he knows better than to fuck up a good thing.' Said something about learning your lesson a long time ago and that you were just distracted by a little problem that she is going to take care of with, and I quote, 'great pleasure.' What does that even mean, Dad?"

"Learned my lesson—? Katie, you didn't happen to overhear what Aunt Fi is planning, did you?" He could not even find Liam to warn him if Fi was planning something terrible.

Katie blinked. "Okay, let me get this straight. You are not grounding me again, right? No matter what I say?" Her words were deliberate. Some day he would need to teach her a thing or two about priorities.

"Katie, this is serious. Tell me."

"She wouldn't say. I swear. She just told Mom not to worry about it and left. Didn't say where she was going or what she was going to do."

Ethan deflated. Fiona was talking about Liam. Did she know about them back then? Liam had paused on her face the night they'd all met in the woods before he had paused on Ethan's. The hesitation that led to him getting shot in the shoulder came from his shock at seeing Fiona. Why hadn't he seen that before?

"Thanks, Katie. You're not grounded, but let's just keep this between us, okay?" He hated himself for asking his only daughter to keep a secret from her mother. None of this was their fault. He never wanted to drag any of them into his world, and now the consequences of his actions threatened to destroy them all.

"Are you cheating on her, Dad?" She looked up at him with big blue eyes, and he regretted lying to her even before he opened his mouth.

"No, baby. Your Aunt Fiona sometimes gets crazy ideas in her head, and she doesn't think them through before she acts on them. Now go on and get out of here."

She begrudgingly obliged, and as soon as the door shut behind her, he poured himself a large drink to wash away the bitter taste of his lies.

ETHAN KNEW all he had to do was get Liam to see reason and talk to him, man to man, and make him look at the photograph—*See, Liam? See? That's us. We were something to each other. All we need to do is remember what we were and how we lost that.*—but, hell, he knew firsthand it was a lot to take in.

They were enemies. Sworn enemies. Liam was a wolf, and Ethan was practically bred to hunt him. He killed Liam's kind, and Liam killed his.

Could they actually have been as madly in love with each other as he felt they were in his dreams, with the real world against them? The list of people who would try any means necessary to break them apart was endless.

He needed to talk to Liam. Threats of death or not, he was not finding answers on his own, and he deserved—no, both of them deserved—to know the truth about their past.

So he started looking again. He went out every night, stayed out until dawn, even drove back to Cocoa to see if there was any sign he had been there, but his searches turned up nothing.

Liam had disappeared.

The dreams didn't stop. They just got darker as the days went on.

Ethan refusing to kill a child wolf as Charles demanded.

Charles threatening Ethan, screaming that he was not his son anymore, damning him, threatening to kill him because a wolf sympathizer was a wolf in his eyes.

Ethan breaking down in his room alone, missing Liam, needing Liam.

Liam backed into a tree by Charles wielding his favorite large knife one night after Charles had killed several others without breaking a sweat, and Ethan panicking and distracting him, risking his own life to save Liam.

The sad look in Liam's eyes as he escaped.

The lies he had to tell his father to keep Liam safe and secret.

Stolen kisses, desperate embraces, sad good-byes—they all swirled together with violent visions of Charles's more creative punishments.

Liam seething with anger when he saw the bruises and welts on Ethan's skin from one of Charles's insane survival sessions.

Ethan holding Liam back out of some sick, unearned loyalty to his only living parent when Liam vowed to tear Charles limb from limb.

Ethan balled up in Liam's arms, crying because he didn't know what else to do. Neither of them could escape. Charles wouldn't let Ethan leave so easily. No Robertson was stepping out on his family. And Liam's family would hunt Liam down if he tried to leave. And even if he did manage it, he would never thrive without them.

But worst of all were the dreams where Fiona would show up. Each one ended with Liam's death. Sometimes an explosion. Sometimes Fiona would stab him in the heart. Sometimes she would force Ethan to kill him and then kill Katie and Jamie. Those were the dreams that made him wake up screaming. Those weren't memories. He feared they were predictions of things to come.

Ethan woke up sobbing now every morning.

It was late on a Friday night weeks later. Moira had left early in the morning for a few days away, citing needing some time to think. She had arranged for Katie to stay at a friend's until Sunday, and Jamie hadn't been home for days. Moira made an unsubtle suggestion that Ethan get his shit together or just get his shit and leave by the time she got back. He couldn't blame her one bit.

He was on his second glass of whiskey and the TV was blaring some show about alien invasions, but Ethan was staring at the clock as the late hours changed into early ones. The demanding knock on the door, arrhythmic but forceful, broke his spell.

It was not an expected sound.

Dressed in ragged jeans and a hooded sweatshirt and leaning against the doorframe like he would fall over otherwise, eyes red rimmed and unfocused, was Liam. He looked the complete opposite of the snarky, composed man he made himself out to be these days. He looked crazed and sad and confused and haunted all at the same time.

Ethan shook his head and started to speak, but Liam lazily held up a finger and whispered, "Shh."

Ethan didn't sense that he was in danger, or that in this state Liam was even capable of being dangerous, but he also could not sense his endgame. He knew if Liam wanted him dead, he would not have been standing there looking so lost.

Liam closed his eyes slowly and bit his lip like he was trying to find the words, and it was several seconds before he breathed out and stared Ethan down. "I—" He stumbled a bit, and Ethan, because he was Ethan, reached out to catch him before he fell.

So close to Liam then, and the sense memories flooded through Ethan.

Liam laughed but it was resigned and resentful. He pursed his lips together and shook his head. He managed two words. Two words without sarcasm or pretext running through them.

"I remember."

And there it was.

CHAPTER 21

WHEN THE shock wore off, Ethan ushered Liam inside and poured him a large glass of whiskey and another for himself.

Liam rolled the glass in his hands, like he was trying to think of exactly what he wanted to say. Ethan let him compose his thoughts, even though his insides were screaming to find out what Liam knew.

After a few long sips, he put the glass down and closed his eyes, fingers curling and uncurling unconsciously. When he finally opened his eyes again, he looked calm. "I'm going to be completely honest with you, Ethan. But I need to know that you'll be honest with me too."

"I will." He set his own glass down and turned to face Liam, but Liam still didn't look at him.

Liam took a deep breath. "How did you know where to find me in Cocoa?"

Ethan sighed. "I wasn't looking for you. Not exactly, anyway. I was looking for... for answers. I kept seeing this place in my dreams and you—"

"I was there in them, wasn't I? We were... together?" There was an undercurrent of excitement running through Liam's voice, like he hadn't trusted his own memory until Ethan confirmed it.

"Yeah. And I don't know why, but I just found myself driving out of town and heading to where I knew that place was. Didn't know how I knew how to get there. And when I was there, I just started walking.

And everything was familiar somehow. I knew every inch of the place. And when I saw you there...." He stopped himself, lost for a moment in the memory of what they had almost done there in the glade.

Liam brought him out of his thoughts. "How long?"

"How long what?" He could still feel Liam's hands exploring his sun-warmed skin there in the clearing.

"How long have you been having these dreams?"

"About two months. Ever since—ever since that first night, I guess. I just thought they were, you know, it's not uncommon to confuse fighting and sex in your subconscious. I dismissed them. At first. But then, you know, I knew something more was going on."

Liam's eyes finally met Ethan's. "I thought you were... I thought you were doing this to me. I thought it was some trick to lure me out in the open. Some kind of spell to get in my head. But these... things I'm seeing... these feelings I have when I see them, see you now, they're real, aren't they? I couldn't kill you that night because something inside *me* told me not to. I almost... we almost... in Cocoa, in your house, because we have before, haven't we?" He kept asking as if he needed Ethan or even himself to justify what was happening.

"A lot, in fact. It's all true, isn't it, Ethan? I wasn't sure, but now I know. Because I *remember*. Fighting on opposite sides again after all these years must have triggered you, and your smell, God, your smell triggered me. It all makes sense now. A few more months and you probably would have remembered on your own, but I can't wait that long." Liam rambled around the point without actually getting to it, and Ethan was getting just a little frustrated.

"Liam, what are you talking about?"

"Don't you see?" Like it was the most obvious thing ever and Ethan was an idiot. "We were so young. The war between us, between our people, it would just get that much worse if someone knew about us. We tried to stay away from each other. We couldn't. We'd swear to stay away from each other, and it would last at most two days before we would be back in each other's...."

Ethan listened to Liam's voice, but the words stopped making sense at some point and a memory flashed in his head. He struggled to connect to it, to make it coherent. There was not much to go on, just feelings, mostly. Unimaginable sadness. Resignation. Loss. Fear. There was the low light of a streetlamp in the darkness and Liam's hands on his. He was crying. Tears fell uncontrollably down his face.

"You see it, don't you?" Liam, the real Liam, inched closer to him and looked him straight in the eye. "Tell me you remember."

"I see…. Oh, God. Oh, God, Liam! *The explosion.*" He closed his eyes tightly and focused on the Liam in his dreams, smiling wistfully through tears, touching Ethan's face, his hands, his chest, like at any moment someone would come and rip Ethan away from him.

"Ethan, it's the only way. I wish it weren't, but—"

"No, Liam, please!" Ethan broke down, hanging his head in his hands.

This was the moment when what little was left of his whole world came crashing down around him. He didn't want to remember this. But the memories attacked him from all sides. Their first meeting, so long ago on the archery field. Their first kiss. Secret plans, midnight meetings, the emotional fight that eventually led to his father's death….

The memories became hazy after that, swirls of fire and smoke and bursts of light, screaming and choking.

When Ethan pulled himself from the memory and opened his eyes, he was weeping.

He raised his hand to his face and touched his lips absentmindedly. The shock of it all ran through him like lightning. It was several minutes before he could find the means to speak.

He took a deep breath. "Well… what do we do now?"

Liam raised an eyebrow. "I honestly don't know."

Neither spoke again for a long time.

When it got awkward, Ethan poured another round of whiskey. He grabbed Liam's glass off the coffee table and offered it to him. His fingers lightly grazed Liam's when he took it, and a small sigh escaped Ethan's lips. He panicked inside and looked to Liam to see if he had heard it. *Of course he heard it, damn wolf hearing.* He looked at Liam for longer than was probably necessary, and Liam wasn't looking away either.

"Thanks," Liam finally said, but he set the glass back down.

Ethan made a noncommittal noise and placed his hands in his lap.

Liam's eyes wandered around the room and landed on a picture of Ethan and Moira at someone's wedding a few years back.

"She's... pretty."

Ethan cleared his throat. "She's not you."

Liam turned his head to look at Ethan. "Does she know?"

He sighed. "No. None of it. She's my wife. I respect her too much to...." *Be thinking about someone else constantly... to tell her just how far I've gone with you in the last month... how much farther I want to go right now....*

"And here you are with me." Ethan didn't miss the little quirk of his eyebrow.

"I know. I won't apologize for it."

"To me or to her?"

He simply shrugged. "She and I make a good team."

"Do you love her?" It was a fair question.

"I love you."

The words spilled out before he could stop them, and before he could backtrack, claim it was the memories talking, Liam lunged off his side of the sofa and crawled on top of Ethan, forcing him to turn and face him. He stopped short, their faces so close he could feel the heat coming off Liam. Ethan was getting hard. Something it took him longer to do with Moira, God help her. God help him too.

Liam's eyes flashed a range of emotions too quickly for Ethan to pick up on any one of them, but when Liam finally spoke, the low growl running under it told him everything he needed to know.

"Still? Even now? Even after all these years? Even after I had to kill—"

Ethan couldn't take it anymore and leaned in to kiss Liam. He felt Liam respond almost immediately. The kiss was soft, exploring, and Ethan felt his whole body shiver like it hadn't since their last night together. He tried to breathe, but Liam deepened the kiss, and he promptly forgot every need except for Liam.

They were hungry, greedy for each other, like they had been drowning all this time and had finally clawed to the surface for air.

What in the hell am I doing? I must be insane. But he didn't stop.

They kissed for a few moments, and Liam pulled back.

"Are you sure about this, Ethan?" Liam looked scared that Ethan was going to come to his senses and stop, but Ethan harbored no such desire.

"I'm sure. I forgave you a long time ago, Liam." He thrust up against Liam just in case his words weren't clear enough.

Liam looked dazed but satisfied with his answer.

He kissed a line down Ethan's throat, unbuttoning his shirt as he went. He stopped at each nipple, biting at them, licking them until Ethan was panting, jerking his hips into Liam and making it very obvious his dick was extremely interested in what was happening there.

Liam kissed farther and farther down until he reached the top of his jeans and looked up at Ethan, with an incredibly turned on look in his eyes. He popped the button open and unzipped them so he could shove them down and off completely, taking his boxers with them.

Liam was still fully dressed, and the contrast made Ethan feel vulnerable and at a disadvantage, but he was not going to break the moment and protest, not when his cock was hard against his belly and Liam was looking at it greedily.

Liam grinned wolfishly and licked a wet stripe from the base to the tip before taking it into his mouth. Ethan shuddered with pleasure, tried to stifle the cry that needed to come out, but when Liam started to take more of him in, he couldn't stop himself.

As if encouraged by the noises, Liam started to move up and down on Ethan. Liam hollowed his cheeks and used his tongue for more sensation. Ethan bucked once, thrusting into his mouth, and Liam pushed back down on him, setting the nerves near his hip bones on fire and making it so much better. He brought him to full hardness in no time at all, brought him close to the edge but not enough to make him go over.

Which meant there was more to come.

Liam pulled off and licked his lips. "Some things never change, do they?"

"Oh my God, Liam." He couldn't see straight. He was so hard and so turned on and so in need of everything Liam, he couldn't focus on anything else.

"I still have it, I see. Good to know. Shall I continue?"

"Oh, God. Yes. Please, Liam. Don't stop now. Please."

"I think, then, we should go upstairs." Liam stood and pulled Ethan to standing as well. He brought Ethan close for a kiss like he couldn't help but have something touching Ethan at all times.

"Tell me you have something," Liam whispered anxiously, almost a prayer, as if he didn't want to know if the answer wasn't yes.

"Yes, yes, of course. My bedroom. In my nightstand." He had been down but not completely out since he was last with Moira.

"Good. Upstairs. Bed."

Liam grabbed Ethan's hand and pulled him along, just like he used to, looking back and grinning, laughing, pulling him harder if he didn't keep up. Liam pushed him down on the bed and then took off his own clothes so they were evenly undressed now. Ethan looked at his form with admiration.

And Liam noticed. "You like?"

Ethan nodded. "Yeah, I like. Different than what I remember. Change is good, though." His eyes swept down to Liam's hard cock.

Liam lay back down across Ethan, this time skin to skin, and Ethan loved the feel of it. They spent a few minutes exploring, rediscovering each other, learning new scars and new, more adult bodies. Neither was the scrawny early twentysomething they had been before, and each new bump of muscle or patch of hair was met with surprise and approval from the other.

Liam reached over into Ethan's nightstand and set about slicking up his fingers nicely with a devilish look in his eyes. He used one hand to stroke Ethan slowly, torturously, making him grip the sheets and curl his toes.

"The first time we did this, I spent so much time making sure you were ready for what was to come. I wanted it to be as pleasant as possible under the circumstances. I won't lie, though. If it's been a while since you did this—"

"I haven't. Not since you and I did this. Unless I made another pact with someone *else* to forget."

Liam smirked a little at the ribbing and shook his head. "It's just like riding a bicycle, Ethan. Even if you've forgotten everything else, your body hasn't. Just relax and let it remember."

Ethan did as he was told, and Liam kept stroking him as he started working him open with his fingers, one at a time, slowly, and carefully.

"Yeah, just like that, Ethan. Just let it happen."

Ethan closed his eyes and lost himself in Liam's reassurances. It felt so good—too good, perhaps. He was shaking, moaning, and hissing through his teeth at every push and stroke.

"Now, don't come yet, Ethan." Liam had three fingers in him, and Ethan was close to tears trying not to come.

Liam pulled them out slowly and reached for the bottle again, coming to his knees to give Ethan a good show of slicking the both of them up. Ethan couldn't breathe, watching Liam fist his own cock. This was actually happening. *I really hope I am not dreaming again.*

Liam lowered himself again, pulled Ethan's legs into a better position, and paused just before pushing in. He guided himself to Ethan and carefully started to enter. Ethan breathed through it, forcing himself to relax and let him in, and it was not long before Liam was buried in him.

Ethan nodded his head after a few seconds to get used to the feeling, and Liam started to pull out and thrust in slowly.

"God, it's been so long since... we could have been... all this time, we could have been... God, this feels so good. So right."

Liam's rambling litany was a good focal point for Ethan while he got used to the movement inside him. Soon the discomfort subsided, and Ethan was gripping Liam's shoulders, scratching at his skin. The nagging sense of loss he had been feeling was replaced by a sense of wholeness, of having missed a part of his body and not just a part of his memory, like Liam being gone was akin to losing a limb.

They fucked like they'd lost no time since their last time together, moving in perfect rhythm with each other, pushing, pulling, all in harmony. Ethan briefly flashed to the memory of Antonio and Sasha in the woods and how they moved together and the insane pangs of jealousy he'd felt watching them. But even as the rift between Liam and him was healing, Ethan knew there were going to be cracks in that repair, because inside those cracks was one hell of a body count.

Ethan came first, another thing about him that hadn't changed, obviously. He had himself in his fist, stroking in rhythm with Liam's thrusts. Liam didn't break eye contact with him as it happened, just gave him breathy words of encouragement. He spilled over his fist and onto his belly, and Liam whispered, "Oh, God, yes," and the sight of Ethan coming must have been a good one, because Liam came soon after, howling noisily before collapsing on top of Ethan.

They broke apart after a few minutes and lay there, touching each other, eventually curling into each other, until they both fell asleep.

CHAPTER 22

THEY WENT twice more before the sun rose, each time better than the last, and Ethan didn't even care that he was going to be sore for *weeks* after that.

They woke up for good in the midmorning and begrudgingly went downstairs for coffee. It was on the second cup that Ethan dared to address the lingering issues on his mind. Or, at least the ones dealing with Liam. The fact that Fiona had known this whole time that they had a past was another matter entirely that he would deal with soon enough.

"When I woke up, I was in the hospital. I'd lost several months of memories they said I might never get back. But, how, I mean, when did you...."

Liam closed his eyes and rolled his head upward. "I assume your memories stop around the time we met, right?"

"Yeah. They said it was—"

"Convenient, is what it is, Ethan. I woke up at my uncle's house in Virginia. No memory of the summer at all. Two people with the same memory loss? That's not normal amnesia. That's magic. Someone took away our memories, don't you see? Someone made us forget and—" He gestured wildly around the room. "You moved on. You have a *family* now. I—"

"Shh...." Ethan grabbed Liam and pulled him close. "We'll figure it out, okay? We found each other after all this time, despite magic or whatever was trying to keep us apart. Do you think we're going to let anything get between us again?"

Ethan kissed Liam, gripped him tightly until he was calmer, and maybe some things had changed because a panicked Liam was an entirely new concept to him.

"We have to keep this to ourselves for now. From my pack and your—your family. My family won't speak to me. They haven't in over twenty years. I only came back because I heard my father was dead, but still I am shut out. They were serious, it seems, when they cast me out. I only joined up with this pack for protection when you brought me here. You see what happens when I am on my own for too long. I'm a strong fighter but new to them, and they will kill me if they know about us, but I have no loyalty to them yet. I can make a clean break. I think the question here is, can you? You have… God, Ethan, you have children."

"Liam, I—my children are nearly grown. I will always be their father no matter what, but how can I be with Moira when I know now that I never really loved her? Part of me wonders if all this… this life I have now… wasn't something manipulated by Fiona. She knows who you are. She didn't forget like I did. She's known all along and chose to keep it from me. I don't think anything here except my feelings for my kids is real. Moira and I haven't spoken for weeks. I honestly think she likes my sister more than me. Liam.…" Ethan kissed him again and again. "Liam, this is what I want. And I will do whatever it takes to get back what we lost twenty-three years ago."

Liam swallowed hard. "I should—I should get back to them. For now, at least. Lay low until we figure this all out."

"Yeah." But Ethan wasn't letting him go.

Liam smiled. "Again? You're going to be the death of me."

"Is that a no?" Ethan buried his head in the crook of Liam's neck and scraped his teeth along the soft skin there.

Liam's head fell back and he groaned, letting Ethan push him back against the table. "Mmmm… right here?" Liam tugged at his shirt.

"Upstairs is too far away." Ethan lifted his arms so Liam could take it all the way off.

He was never gladder Moira had insisted on the more expensive dining room table than the moment he crawled on top of it and a reclining Liam without it giving a single wobble.

Liam was hard under his jeans, no foreplay needed as Ethan unzipped him and took him in his mouth. His cock was hot and heavy as he swirled his tongue around it, loving the noises Liam made and the way he clenched his fists.

He took his time, enjoying Liam's reactions—his hitched breaths and whimpers, the way his muscles tightened when Ethan knew he just wanted to thrust up into his mouth. He felt twenty again, even if just for the moment, and he wanted to make it last because he knew what would happen next and he just didn't want to face it yet.

Liam pulled Ethan up so he could stretch across him. "So good. But I want to be able to fuck you one last time before I go, okay? Want to bend you over this table and fuck you so hard you don't forget me again."

"I could never. I'm not letting you get away from me ever again. I don't care what we have to do to be safe, but I swear to you that we will be together."

"Oh, for *fuck's sake.* Are you fucking kidding me?"

The new voice rang loudly across the room.

Fiona.

Ethan and Liam scrambled to their feet. Her keys, spare house keys he regretted ever letting her have in the first place, fell out of her hand.

"Jesus *Christ*, Ethan! You just couldn't stay away, could you? And *you*, Kinnaird." She spat out the word like it was poison. "You just can't die, can you?"

"*Fiona—*"

"No! You don't get to speak, Ethan! Everything I did for you! For Dad! I thought—we thought—you were just young and stupid and it was some kind of fucked-up phase, but now? You have a wife and children, and after everything I did, you're right back here in the arms of the monster that killed our father? You're not even supposed to— Fuck! Do we really mean so little to you that you have to act on your sick urges to fuck a wolf? A wolf, mind you, that just won't *stay dead* no matter how many times I've tried!"

Ethan opened his mouth, but it was Liam who spoke first. His voice was low, accusing. "It *was* you. Wasn't it? The warehouse that night. You were the one who triggered the explosion."

Ethan whipped around to Liam and then turned to Fiona. He knew his sister was sick, but this was beyond anything he'd thought she was capable of, especially at fifteen. "Fiona?"

Fiona smiled, and it was horrible. "How else was I supposed to find this *thing*? You were hiding out pretty well after you *killed my father*, weren't you, Liam? But I knew you two couldn't stay away from each other, you sick *fucks*. All I had to do was wait for the phone call from one of the hunters you abandoned when you betrayed our family that night. You think I didn't have your ass tailed all day long, big brother? You led us right to him. You think Grandma and Grandpa could keep me there for long?"

"So, what was I, then? Collateral damage?"

"Awwwww, Ethan, *sweetie*." Fiona reached out her hand to caress his cheek, but Ethan batted it away. Fiona didn't even flinch. "You were what you've been for as long as I've known you. *Useless*."

Fiona's eyes narrowed, and Ethan wondered if he would be able to live with himself if he killed her right here in his house.

"But you lived. You both lived. My mistake, I guess. I've learned a lot since then, you know. Won't happen again, I can promise you that."

The shotgun cock registered in Ethan's brain before he saw it. His closest weapon was a room away. They had no other choice.

She threw Ethan silver chains and motioned for him to tie Liam to a chair. They both knew she would kill Ethan if Liam tried to escape. He finished up and reluctantly sat so Fiona could tie him up in a similar fashion with heavy rope.

"They came to me, your family. Had the *balls* to come to the hospital after the explosion. They finagled me into my biggest mistake that night: a truce. Me, can you imagine it? Said I could get my brother back and everything could go back to normal if I agreed to leave them alone. They said I should leave town just to make sure. They would not attack us, and we wouldn't attack them. And, as a bonus, they would make it so you two wouldn't remember each other. *Nepenthe*, they called it. Ancient magic to take away your memories, take away your sorrows—take away all our sorrows, right? And if I said no? They kill you and me and Grandma and Grandpa."

She had been rummaging through her bag as she spoke, and she finally retrieved her prize—silver rods with flared tips. Without a second thought, she shoved them deep into Liam's shoulders until they embedded in the thick wood of the chair behind him. He screamed, and Ethan fought against his own restraints, but he wasn't strong enough to break them.

Fiona went back to her bag like nothing had happened.

"So I said yes. Any guilt I felt at trying to kill you was erased, and I had the chance at a normal life with my brother. And your indiscretion was history. I watched one of them destroy your memories of Liam like he was putting a bandage on a paper cut. For the best, right? There are always other packs to hunt.

"And after you recovered, they came to me again, and I assured them that their magic worked and that I would convince you to leave town as soon as you were physically capable. It was so easy. We never again had a reason to go back. Everything was perfect. Until I heard rumors that a mess of a coven actually managed to take down an elder wolf at home. Your old man, Liam. Gotta respect them for that, right? I wasn't going to bother going home to get in the middle of *that*, though. Who cares if a few witches take out a wolf or two, right? Hell, I'd probably offer to help."

She sighed and rolled her eyes. She looked fifteen again. Except the hints of a sadistic streak Ethan saw in her so long ago had burst through to the surface. There was nothing left of the Fiona he knew then. She had become worse than Charles could ever imagine being. She had surpassed his cruelty, his vengeance, his pride in every way possible.

"Fiona, you don't have to do this! Please!" Every nightmare of Fiona killing Liam was coming true and there was nothing he could do.

Fiona didn't react. Ethan was sure she was so manic and crazed that she couldn't even hear him.

"But then they started killing *humans*. You know, things that *matter*. But taking you, Ethan, was *never* part of the plan. I didn't want to risk triggering a memory after all these years. They said it might happen as time went on, especially seeing places from your past, but the last thing I was expecting that night was to see *you*."

She turned to Liam and shoved the gun barrel to his chest. He was pale and sweating. The blood gushed from his wounds.

"And here we are. Everything would have been fine if you had just not insisted on going that night, big brother. I told you it was nothing I couldn't handle, didn't I? But you had to stick your nose in it, and look at us now." She shook her head with mock sadness sliding across her face.

"This time there's no escaping death. I've been waiting twenty-three years to kill you, Liam. And Ethan, you would have lived if you hadn't gone back to him. I hope all this was worth it."

"What did you do, Fiona?" Ethan looked up at his sister.

She sucked in a breath through her teeth and gave him a condescending smile. "Gas leaks are terrible things, aren't they? And what is Moira going to say when she finds out that you died with a wolf in the house? What will Katie and Jamie say? I hear losing a parent can do *really crazy things* to a kid. Perhaps make them better killers. Aunt Fi's favorite niece and nephew, killing by her side. Seeking revenge for turning their father into a wolf-fucker? Seeking to right the dishonor you brought on them? They'll be *fantastic*. I did always say I'd be the cool aunt."

"You leave my kids alone! They have *nothing* to do with this!" He fought against the restraints again.

Fiona walked over to him and kissed him on the forehead. "Good-bye, big brother." She smiled, sickeningly sweet, and went to get her things. "I'll give you one consolation, Ethan. I'm going outside to set this thing in motion. Luckily for you, it'll probably be, oh, ten minutes before, you know...." She made an explosion sound and punctuated it with a hand gesture. "If you have something to say to this... thing... now is the time to get it all out."

She started to put away her shotgun.

Which made the gunshot they heard a split second later that much more surprising.

CHAPTER 23

FIONA FROZE, but it was too late. Blood gushed from the wound to her right shoulder and she fell to the floor. Ethan looked around the room wildly to see where the shot had come from, and from the corner of his eye, he caught wild curls running toward him from the living room.

Katie. And behind her, Jamie.

"Katie! What did you…? How did you…?"

Katie dropped the gun and set about untying him. Jamie went to where Fiona was crumpled on the ground. Ethan could see the pool of blood from where he was, and it was getting bigger.

"She'll live. It's a clean shot." Jamie was almost too clinical in his reactions. He started basic first aid to slow the bleeding. "I'll take care of her, Dad."

There was a network of people to go to when going to a hospital would raise too many questions. It was one of the ways the Robertsons had made it that far without giving away their secrets.

Ethan's mind raced in a million different directions. "No. Call Dr. Campbell. He'll take care of her. Number's in my phone on the counter there."

Jamie nodded and made the call.

Gideon Campbell had been a hunter once. He'd lost his wife, Narcissa, and son, William, to a particularly nasty pack back in the seventies. He quickly found his niche in field triage and used his credentials as a dentist as an excuse to carry medical equipment that had secretly saved many lives.

"Better get this guy loose before it's too late." Katie finished with the rope holding Ethan and pulled him to standing.

"Katie. Jamie. I don't understand...."

The rods were still holding Liam to the chair, and Fiona had made damn sure removing them would be as painful as possible. The only thing to do was pull him so they went all the way through. Answers could wait.

He approached Liam gingerly. This wasn't a normal injury. This wasn't a wooden arrow to the chest or a stab wound from a kitchen knife.

"There's no other way. I'm sorry."

Liam was pale and shaky. He could only nod his head to let Ethan know he understood. The silver was quickly poisoning him, and he didn't have much time.

Ethan took a deep breath. He loosened the length of silver chain so it fell at Liam's feet and then grasped Liam by the back of his shoulders. Liam whimpered the moment Ethan touched the rod. Ethan trembled slightly, knowing how much pain he was about to cause Liam.

"Do it. Do it. Do it. Get them out. Please." It was no more than a whisper.

Ethan pulled, and Liam groaned. He could feel the metal grind against bone.

"Dad, you need to hurry." Katie had joined him. "Let's... let's do it on three, okay? I'll get this side."

"You'd save an enemy?" He'd never wanted this. He'd never wanted this for his own children. Katie was fourteen and needed to be thinking of friends and shopping and school, not war and enemies and destiny and how to disable her own aunt without killing her.

"I'm not sure who the enemy is anymore." She glanced toward Fiona.

Jamie lifted her up, and it was not tender. Fiona cried out from the pain and collapsed in Jamie's arms.

Ethan and Katie ignored her cries and turned back toward Liam, but neither could ignore the sound of Jamie dragging the heavy rope that had just been around Ethan across the floor toward Fiona.

"Okay, baby. On three." So much blood. So much violence. No matter what happened afterward, he was getting his kids out of this for good.

Liam's entire body went taut as Ethan and Katie pulled him through the length of the rods. It was a macabre, horrible sight, but they couldn't stop now. Liam tried to scream, but his body finally succumbed to the shock and pain, and he passed out just before the ends of the rods pushed through him.

When Liam was finally free, Ethan gently set him on the floor and ran to grab anything to help stop the bleeding. He raced back with towels—Moira's Egyptian cotton, if he cared. Liam was stirring, moaning and struggling to take shallow breaths.

"Liam! Liam! Wake up, okay? I need to know if you're healing. Oh, God! Liam! Talk to me, okay?" The room was spinning around him.

Liam opened his eyes, but they were unfocused, glazed over. "Ethan?"

Ethan touched his face. "Yeah. Yeah, Liam. I'm right here. I'm not going anywhere. But you gotta tell me, okay? You need to let me know if you're healing."

Liam tried to swallow. "Not healing."

Fuck. Ethan pulled away one of the towels to see the hole that ran completely through him was, indeed, not shrinking. The bones and tendons were broken and torn. The muscle was destroyed. He had no use of his arms like that.

"What do we do, Dad? Is he dying?" Katie sounded as panicked as Ethan felt.

Ethan lowered his head, touched his forehead to Liam's. It was cold, colder than a normal human's skin should be, much less a werewolf's. The blood loss was probably too great. "I don't know, Katie. I honestly don't know."

He had just found him again, damn it. And now he was losing him again. The thought was too overwhelming.

"Liam, what do I do?" he whispered.

Liam mouthed something over and over. The noise in the room was too loud for him to hear it.

"Liam, please. What do you need?" He leaned in a little closer until it made sense.

He was saying one word again and again: "Spell."

The healing spell.

"Will it work?" He'd offer his own life for just a tiny bit of hope.

"Don't know. Long shot?" He wheezed as he tried to talk.

Probably the longest, considering the nature of Liam's injuries then, but he would take it.

Ethan grabbed Katie, made her take his place on Liam's wounds, and ran to the garage.

He kept a small dose of the oil he'd used before and had hidden it in a vial in one of his quivers just in case he ever needed it again. He didn't know why at the time and considered burning it along with all the other evidence that Liam was ever there, but he was glad he hadn't listened to that urge.

Ethan hurried back, his chest aching from the stress as he set everything up for the spell. It worked before. It had to work again now. He motioned for Katie to stand back, and he started the spell.

His hands shook as he read from the pages and doused Liam's wound with the oil. He lost focus on everything around him save Liam and his own words. This wasn't the sick grab for answers like the first time he'd performed it. The stakes were infinitely higher. He concentrated on every word, making sure he got them right.

When it was over, all he could do was wait.

Gideon Campbell arrived soon after and didn't ask any questions before running to Fiona and properly attending to her wound. He had a full surgery bay tucked away in his offices if she needed it. Ethan couldn't bring himself to care enough about her well-being to ask if she did, considering how much she cared for his.

He wouldn't take his eyes off Liam, watching his face, his skin, his wounds for any change, good or bad.

Katie did not leave his side. The memory of Ethan's first kill kept running through his head. He was fourteen, just like Katie. He'd come upon a wounded wolf in the forest, and it was a grotesque sight. He was half-turned and whimpering, bleeding from deep, long gashes to his major arteries. Ethan knew that no pack would leave a wolf to die in such a terrible way and that he must have been an omega, alone and suffering. The wolf caught sight of Ethan and had reached out for him.

"Please." He wasn't asking for help. He was asking for death.

Ethan only hesitated a moment before putting the wolf out of his misery, swiftly and painlessly. He was okay until three nights later when it finally hit him that he had taken a life. His first kill had been a mercy kill, but still it haunted him for months afterward. He had trouble sleeping and eating. He lost twenty pounds he didn't have to lose those first three months.

Ethan pulled his daughter close. If a mercy killing had messed him up so badly, how would shooting a family member, even an evil one, affect her?

Jamie joined them after a few minutes, putting his hand on Ethan's shoulder gently to get his attention.

"Dr. Campbell is taking Fiona to his office. She's… she's going to be okay. He needs to stitch her up and get her on antibiotics, but he doesn't think the bullet hit anything major. He wants to talk to you, though."

Ethan looked down at Liam again. He didn't want to leave him, even for a second.

"Dad, it's okay. We're not going to let anything happen to him." He had trained his kids well. There was no way they hadn't seen just what Liam meant to him, just what Liam was, and they were still offering to help him.

Ethan rubbed his face and stood. There was so much blood everywhere. He was too old for this.

"Thanks for coming, Gideon."

He had dosed Fiona with something strong and fast-acting. She looked peaceful despite everything, despite who she really was.

Gideon tilted his head toward Liam and raised a questioning eyebrow. "I'm going to pull my car into the garage so we won't arouse any suspicion. Why don't you walk me out there and tell me just what I've gotten myself into here."

He listened to Ethan's story. There was no reason not to start from the beginning. It was all out there now. There was no going back after today anyway. He was only sorry that Moira was going to get hurt in this fallout.

Gideon was silent for a long time after Ethan got to the end of it.

When he did speak, it was deliberate and calculated. "Ethan, I've been at this a long time. A very long time. There have always been rumors about the way your family operates outside the rules, but no one could ever get confirmation. Your father had a tight grip on his people, and Fiona even more so. This is"—he breathed in sharply—"this is insane, what you're telling me right now. She tried to kill her own brother? Twice?"

"Gideon, I know it's hard to believe, but—"

"And you, son. What were you thinking, taking up with a wolf? Do you know how bad this looks right now?"

Ethan sighed. "Yeah, Gideon. I do. Is there a precedent for this? Human and wolf? Robertson and Kinnaird? I mean, I'm not an outsider who happened to join the fight. And he's not a random wolf. Have you ever heard of this?"

"If it's happened, they've buried it deep." Gideon blew out a breath and looked down. "Okay. Okay, kiddo. We can fix this. Fiona's not going far in her condition. Ethan—Ethan, there are safeguards in place to take care of rogues like this. They're not pleasant, and you'll probably never see her again, but if your story is true…."

Ethan had heard of these safeguards. People like Fiona ended up in psychiatric facilities, heavily sedated for the rest of their lives. The punishment used to be instant death, but he was not sure the modern way was a step up or three steps back. But as long as Fiona ran free, he and everyone he loved was in danger.

He didn't think twice. "Do it. Call whoever you need. She was planning to blow up the house and make it look like a gas explosion. I'm sure she left enough proof around here to back up my story."

Gideon put a fatherly hand on his shoulder, and Ethan wished, not for the first time, that someone like Gideon had been his father instead of Charles. "Just make sure you're doing this for the right reasons, Ethan."

He thought of Liam and the time they had lost and what they still stood to lose if he didn't pull through. "I am, Gideon."

He nodded. "I'll make the call as soon as I get her stabilized, but, Ethan, you really need to think about what you're taking on if you continue down this path." Gideon's entire family dead by wolves, and still there was no anger or hurt in his voice at Ethan's supposed betrayal to the cause. Gideon was only concerned for Ethan's well-being. Ethan thought of him and Tim and countless others he'd encountered over the years, and suddenly realized that only Charles and Fiona had been so rigid in their lack of forgiveness and tolerance.

"I can't think of anything else but, Gideon."

Gideon shook his head and got into his car to back it into the garage. Ethan opened the door for him and made his way into the kitchen.

His heart stopped when, above the din of Gideon's engine and the grinding metal of the garage door, he heard a beautiful sound.

"Ethan?"

Tears sprang to his eyes as he ran to Liam, still on the floor. Katie and Jamie were still there with him, redressing the wounds that had started to stitch back together. His color had started to come back, but he still looked weak and exhausted.

"Liam!"

"Ethan. How are we doing? Did we win?" He hissed as Jamie moved his arm so it would reset better.

"You're going to be all right. That's a win in my book." He touched Liam's face, and Liam closed his eyes.

"Good. Good." He drifted in and out of consciousness for a minute or two before going out completely.

Ethan sat back and looked at his children. They all had a lot of explaining to do.

They moved Liam to the guest bed to let him sleep it off, and the three of them started mopping up the blood in the kitchen together. It was several minutes before Ethan broke the silence.

"Thank you, guys. We'd be…. I'd be…. If you two hadn't…. Why were you here, anyway?"

Jamie rolled his eyes. "You know how Katie is always getting in trouble for snooping and eavesdropping?"

"Yeah?" Ethan had the feeling Katie's bad habit had just become something he could never use against her again.

Jamie looked toward his little sister with something Ethan could almost call pride. "Well, I don't think you should ever ground her again for it. Mom dropped her off at Camilla's house, and she woke up early this morning and got bored and happened to walk by Camilla's parents' room. She overheard her dad, Roger, talking on the phone, and he said your name. Turns out it was Fiona on the other end, spouting off something crazy, and Roger was trying to talk her down.

"She said Roger kept telling her she was acting crazy and needed to calm down before she did something stupid. Katie got scared and tried calling you, but you didn't pick up, so she called me. I was pretty far away, but I raced over to pick her up and we came straight here. We saw the door was open and heard Fiona yelling about killing you, and that's when Katie went for the shotgun you keep in the hall closet."

Katie finally chimed in. "Dad, is what Aunt Fiona said true?"

Ethan breathed in. "How much did you hear, baby?" This was a moment he didn't want to face.

"Did you and he...?" She motioned toward the remaining blood where Liam had been. "Were you...?"

Ethan walked over to her and cupped her face with his hands. "Sweetheart, the next few months are going to be very difficult. I need to speak with your mom before anyone else, but I need you to know that I will always love you and your brother. And even your mom. Always. No matter what happens now, she gave me you and Jamie, and for that I will be grateful to her for the rest of my life."

There were tears in Katie's eyes as she nodded.

"Katie, Jamie, if there's one thing I need you to know about me, it's that I follow our rules. You've known that for as long as you've known about our people. If you don't understand anything else about this, know that the last thing I would do is knowingly put you two in danger by bringing someone unsafe into my life."

"No, but it turns out we've had someone like that our entire lives, haven't we?"

It was starting to hit Katie. Ethan recognized the signs. The trauma was over and now she could absorb everything, and how he handled it would determine how well she did. Charles had never understood the gravity of taking a life, even an enemy's life, and why it affected Ethan so much. He teased him, mocked him, made him feel worthless when he would wake up screaming in the middle of the night. Ethan wouldn't make the same mistakes with his own children.

He held his daughter close and motioned for Jamie to join them. "Kids, what happened today started a long time ago, when your grandfather was still alive. He was a terrible, terrible man, and Fiona worshipped him. I was lucky enough to have your grandmother in my life to balance out his evil, but Fiona never really knew her.

"Grandma was an amazing woman. A lot like your mom, in fact. She kept Charles—your grandfather—in line. When she died, he went off the deep end. Started killing for the fun of it. It wasn't the wolves' fault. She fell asleep at the wheel one night coming home from a friend's house. Charles said she just wanted a break. She went for a night out with friends and left us with a babysitter while he was out hunting. By the time the police found him to tell him she had been in an accident, she was dead. He never got to say good-bye. He blamed the wolves for taking him away from his family so much. Fiona was just a baby when this happened, so she only saw the bad side of him. I love my sister very much, and there was good in her once, but it's too late for her now. Turning her over to Gideon, no matter what she's done, was not an easy decision. But it will keep you two safe."

They cleaned up the rest of the kitchen in silence.

HOURS LATER and Liam was still sleeping peacefully. His wounds were nearly healed by then. Katie was taking a much-needed shower, and Jamie had gone off to his girlfriend's apartment to bring back some of his stuff. Ethan knew it was because he wanted to be there for his sister and mother when Moira came home and everything came out, but he wouldn't say no to having both his children close to him that night, after everything.

Ethan sat on his front porch, whiskey in hand, wondering what the future was going to hold with so many changes coming.

He was so lost in thought he didn't notice he had a guest until an unfamiliar, unexpected weight joined him on the swing.

"You truly love him, don't you, Ethan?"

Oh, fuck me. I can't even. Do you love him?

It only sort of registered that it wasn't Fiona talking. He turned to his mystery guest. She was about thirty, with dark gold hair and an inquisitive look on her face. She didn't feel like a threat to him.

"Hmmmm?"

"You risked your family, your honor, your life. For him. For love."

He couldn't deal with confusion right then. "I'm sorry, but who are you? Do I know you?"

She extended a hand, and he absentmindedly shook it. "Heather. Heather Kinnaird. Liam is my big brother." She had Liam's intelligent eyes and coy smile.

Ethan immediately pulled back. Word traveled fast in the supernatural world, or they'd been keeping tabs on him all along.

Heather must have sensed his distress. "Gideon Campbell is getting old. He's not as inconspicuous or stealthy as he was in his heyday. Heard you saved my brother's life today. Where did you learn that spell?"

"I—Liam got stabbed... in the woods. I used it then. Found him almost dead. Called in a favor."

"So this is a pattern, you going against your family and not killing an innocent man, then?"

"I'm not—" *My father. My sister. A killer. A hunter.* "I'm just... not."

"We know. And you still haven't answered my question."

He looked at Heather. "I'm sorry?"

"My brother. Do you love him? After everything that's happened. After turning on your own family—twice—destroying your marriage and your reputation, do you love Liam?"

Tell me, brother. Do you love him?

He smiled and looked her straight in the eye. He could finally answer the question Fiona had asked twenty-three years ago. "Yeah.

Yeah, I do. I always have. If you really knew my story, you would know that I was ready to give up everything in 1991 to be with him. It was Fiona who put a stop to that."

"Are you still willing to give it all up now? Ethan, we have no real quarrel with you. You've never broken our treaties. You've never killed beyond the scope of the laws. We've been at peace with you for over two decades. We do give Fiona credit for keeping to that, but we have the chance now to strike a real accord for the right reasons."

"The right reasons being…."

"Ethan, my father is dead. My mother is old, and my brothers and sisters have a sibling out here, the eldest sibling, who hasn't been a part of us in far too long. We have a chance now to put things to rights. In our father's absence, we have come to realize that we need Liam. Our parents cast him out all those years ago, and time has softened our mother's feelings on the matter. We have the chance to continue living in peace so our children are safe. We can offer the same to you and your children."

Ethan shook his head. "I won't give up Liam. I didn't find him after all this time just to lose him again."

Heather laughed. "You saved my brother. More than once. Not a million men could hope to break what you have with him. It was never even a thought in my mind to keep you apart. Although we're not crazy that you're a human, on the whole, I guess it could be a lot worse."

"Then what are you offering, and what do you want from me in exchange?" Ethan was understandably wary.

"Ethan, we want our brother back. He is destined to rule our pack, and we aren't whole without him. I have a feeling he is as bonded to you as you seem to be with him. All we ask is that you bring him home. In exchange, we are offering something no wolf has ever offered to a human in our history."

"And what is that, may I ask?" Ethan's heart raced.

"Simple, Ethan. We offer our blessing. We offer our acceptance. Bring Liam home. Let him join us. He can have his own, separate life with you if that's what he wants, but we need him. And I don't think he's going to go without you. He's been lost since our father cast him out all those years ago. It's time for him to come home. Our threats don't come from just humans. Danger is all around. My father died at the hands of one of these threats. And the covens, the other creatures that run the forests and the swamps, they don't stop with us, as you know. Humans have died too."

"You want to… you want to join up? Make peace once and for all and fight on the same side? Protect our home together?" It couldn't be that simple, could it?

"We can't change everyone in the world still fighting this stupid war, but we can change ourselves and maybe start something incredible. Is it so hard to imagine?"

Ethan took a sip of his drink. "You know something, Heather? It isn't. It really isn't."

She grinned. "Do we have an accord?"

"One condition of my own, though."

She raised an eyebrow, and she was definitely Liam's sister with that look on her face.

"This new pack in town. If I'm leaving here, and Fiona is gone, it's going to be hard for the others to take care of it while they regroup. I need to know my kids are safe… I need to know Moira's going to be safe."

She pursed her lips in thought. "Ah, yes. Bunch of punk kids. Shouldn't be too hard. Get him home, and we'll take care of that. As long as we can count on your help with our coven problem. Agreed?"

Something bothered Ethan, though. "Why did your family offer this the first time to Fiona? You could have killed her, me, and anyone else who got in your way that night."

Heather chewed on her bottom lip. "Isn't it obvious? We were losing. Killing you and Fiona that night would have just incited further fights from your allies, and we didn't have the manpower left to defend ourselves. Charles saw to that. We couldn't let on that we were weak, though. My parents saw the opportunity to take out Charles—and punish Liam. They hoped with him gone, it would weaken all of you as well. They knew they were justified in killing Charles that night. The attacks on our people leading up to that night were enough of a reason alone. We didn't provoke him in any way. He came after us.

"And then the explosion happened. Liam was barely hurt. You got the worst of it. They knew that such an act was a sign of desperation and panic, and that it was the perfect time to strike with the idea of a truce. It was supposed to give us time to grow stronger, to add to our pack and grow strong again, and also to separate you and Liam and hide him from Fiona, but after a few years of quiet, we started to like it. No threat we faced in that time was stronger than your family. We took all of them down quickly. Until now."

"So you need me too. Kind of a 'keep your enemies close' thing? Enemy of my enemy and all that?"

She grinned. "You have to admit it kind of benefits everyone all around. You get my brother, just like you want. We get our brother back and gain a human ally. One who can recruit and train to work with us instead of against us. We protect each other from threats so we can all live. Ethan, our families have been fighting for a millennium. Isn't it time we step back and ask ourselves if we're still at it because we truly are enemies or if we have just never been told it's okay to stop? There are rogue packs of wolves out there. Witches. Creatures we've not even encountered yet. And they are ruthless, senseless, and will stop at nothing until wolves and humans alike are dead. Now, I ask you again. Agreed?"

She offered her hand again, and this time Ethan took it enthusiastically. "Agreed."

IT WAS almost dawn when he was finally able to crawl into bed. He opted to sleep next to Liam, curling protectively around him until sleep overtook the trepidation of having to deal with the last loose ends. The biggest being his wife.

He woke up a few hours later to Liam stroking his back. The sun streamed in through the window, and it must have been nearing noon.

He looked up at Liam and smiled.

Liam smiled back, but it was a wary one. "What?"

"How are you feeling?" He wanted to explode with all the news.

Liam stretched a bit experimentally. "Like I fell off a cliff into a meat grinder, but it's a vast improvement from yesterday."

"Everything is a vast improvement from yesterday." Ethan finally had the chance to be the mysterious one.

Liam struggled to sit up for a few moments but ultimately succeeded. "What's that supposed to mean?"

Ethan leaned over and kissed Liam, not caring about morning breath or that he-almost-died-yesterday breath. "Could you eat? Coffee? We have a lot to talk about." He wasn't going to be able to make it long before he exploded with his secret. Everything was just so great at that moment.

Liam raised an eyebrow but nodded.

While Liam took care of his basic needs in the bathroom, Ethan called Heather. They agreed to tell him together, to see that there was no trickery or threat involved.

Twenty minutes later, Liam walked into Ethan's office and saw Ethan and his baby sister, the first family he had seen in years, with a smile on her face.

Liam looked from Ethan to Heather a few times in confusion and shock, but Heather broke the silence and ran to Liam with tears of joy streaming down her face. She threw herself at her big brother and hugged him tightly. Liam looked at Ethan with tears in his own eyes and mouthed a silent "Thank you" as he hugged her back.

He agreed to everything before Ethan had finished pouring the coffee.

Telling Moira, however, was much more difficult than he'd ever imagined.

Liam went on ahead with Heather, and Ethan planned to join him in a few days, once everything had calmed down.

Moira walked in Sunday night and immediately knew something was wrong. There was no good news to balance out Fiona's insanity and his infidelity.

She took in everything about as well as he could have expected. It was painful to watch the heartache bloom across her face as he told her of Liam and their story that had started when he was only twenty. He told her of Fiona's involvement and her attempts on his life and just how dangerous she really was. When he got to Katie and Jamie and what they had done, what Katie had done, she was weeping.

"What have we done to our children, Ethan?" He wanted to hold her, comfort her, but he didn't want to add to the confusion and give her the wrong idea.

"Nothing we can't fix, Moira. We can stop it now. I never wanted to be a hunter. I certainly never wanted to raise my children in this lifestyle. Fiona manipulated every aspect of our lives, and now we have the chance to get the kids away from all of this and let them live normally. You can start over. You can leave this supernatural mess behind if you want to."

"So this is it? We're over? You're giving up on us and your entire life as a hunter for him?"

"Moira, I'm sorry. I'm sorry about all of this." It was just not fair to either of them to pretend to be something he was not.

It was another long night that ended with him crashing on the guest bed. He and Moira, after hours of awkwardness and tears, finally agreed to sort out the details as they came up. For now, she got the house. Despite her family being quite well off, he agreed not to abandon her financially. He had more respect for her than that.

He packed his essentials and left the next night.

He felt every conflicting pair of emotions he could imagine as he drove the long stretch of highway south. Sadness. Happiness. Heartache. Joy. Alone. Loved. But, most of all, he felt something he hadn't felt since the night his father had died.

He felt free.

EPILOGUE

An epilogue… of sorts.

MONTHS PASSED. Ethan and Liam settled into a nice life about a half hour out of town, near the headwaters of the swamp and its forests. It was a large piece of land, private, surrounded by woodlands. Liam was free to let out the wolf as he needed to, and he and Ethan were free to live their lives as they pleased. Ethan committed to keeping the business up north and had even begun to plan for an expansion to the center of the state near his new-old home.

It was a lazy weekend when Ethan surprised Liam with a trip to their spot in Cocoa, for old times' sake and to celebrate.

Working together, they had managed to recover a great deal more memories—some good, some bad. But they had made a lot of new memories too.

The coven was no longer. Most were dead. A few still lived, but the one-two punch of wolf strength and human weapons made them scatter to the wind.

Katie split her time between Ethan and Moira. Ethan and Moira decided together to get Katie some therapy to help her deal with what had happened, and she was doing just fine. Jamie was around a lot more often after he decided to go to college in Tampa. Ethan was not a bit disappointed when he announced he had decided to major in medicine.

Things would always be shaky with Moira, but she eventually came to accept it was over. He heard from Katie that she had even started dating.

"A hunter?"

She giggled a bit before answering. "No, Dad. A *pharmacist*. A real one too. I checked him out. He's... *boring*. But Mom likes him and he does hunt boar and deer and stuff, so Mom doesn't have to hide her .700 and ammo."

"This pharmacist have a name?" He did still care about Moira. He wanted her to be safe and happy. She deserved to be as happy as he was.

"Yeah, a real boring one too, to go with his complete boringness. Kevin. Kevin Hughes. Ugh, right? She met him at some wellness expo thingy." Katie crossed her eyes.

Ethan had to laugh at the absurdity of it all.

No one had heard from or seen Fiona. There were rumors of a psych ward in New Jersey, but no one wanted to open up that wound again. Liam's mother offered to perform the Nepenthe spell once, a thank you for bringing Liam home. Ethan briefly considered it before ultimately deciding that to live with her fate, to live with her sorrows and guilt and the consequences of her actions, it was a punishment she must endure. Making her forget was the easy way out.

It was a warm, sunny day, and they lay on the soft grass and wildflowers just like they used to. Liam laughed softly as Ethan pulled out his phone and turned on the camera.

"Seriously, Ethan?" He propped himself up on his elbows.

"Yeah, I mean, I don't want to forget again, in case we get stupid. Honestly, I don't think we would be here right now if I hadn't hidden that picture I took the first time."

"I think our days of being stupid are over, Ethan. I'm not keen to forget you again anytime soon."

"Would you just indulge me? It's a celebration!"

Liam rolled his eyes but dropped back beside Ethan as he positioned the phone above their heads looking down.

He touched the screen to take the picture and brought it down to look at the result.

The people in the picture were on the ground, and the warm yellow sunlight illuminated the summer wildflowers around them.

One person was looking up at the camera. Ethan, older now, with touches of gray in his hair.

And a now lighter-haired, blue-eyed man who was, instead, gazing at Ethan with a look of such intense affection it made Ethan's jaw drop.

HISTORICAL NOTE

STRUAN ROBERTSON, our brave eleventh-century wolf slayer, was a real man. He did indeed use his small *sgian-dubh* to kill a wolf—a regular wild wolf—that threatened the King.

While the Struan in *Playing Hard To Forget* ignited a millennium-long war with werewolves, the real Struan accepted the gifts of land and title from the King and went on to have children… and those children had children… and those children had children. And on it went for a thousand years, until one day a descendant of that Robertson line produced the author of this book.

Thanks, Great-great-great… some more greats… Grandpa Struan. And thanks to a millennium of Robertsons and kin who kept his story alive.

And a great big thanks to the Liam to my Ethan: JPL. I did this for you.

PIPER DOONE is the red-headed, left handed, and Scottish child of hippies. She had the typical small hippie commune/big city dreams childhood and decided her big dream was to work for Disney, where she learned to live off 30 cents a week after rent, food, and tuition.

She then managed to stumble into a ten-year career in professional sports that lasted ten years too long. She now works a more reasonable job in professional sports marketing, which is far less dangerous actually doing sports.

You can sometimes catch her with her cameras. She shoots digitally and on film and some of her cameras date back to the 1940s. She'd like to say she's a serious photographer with journalism awards and stuff, but she's been featured in exactly one gallery in New York and the photos were of a cow on her farm and a close up of grapes, so, yeah, she's not going down in history there. Other times you can find her with her trusty bow and arrows. Being a Scottish ginger archer, she's heard every Brave joke you can imagine, thank you.

She hates long walks on the beach, sunshine, and summertime, so obviously she lives with her husband, two kids, three hedgehogs, and a dog in sunny, beachy Miami now.

You can find her on Twitter or Facebook.

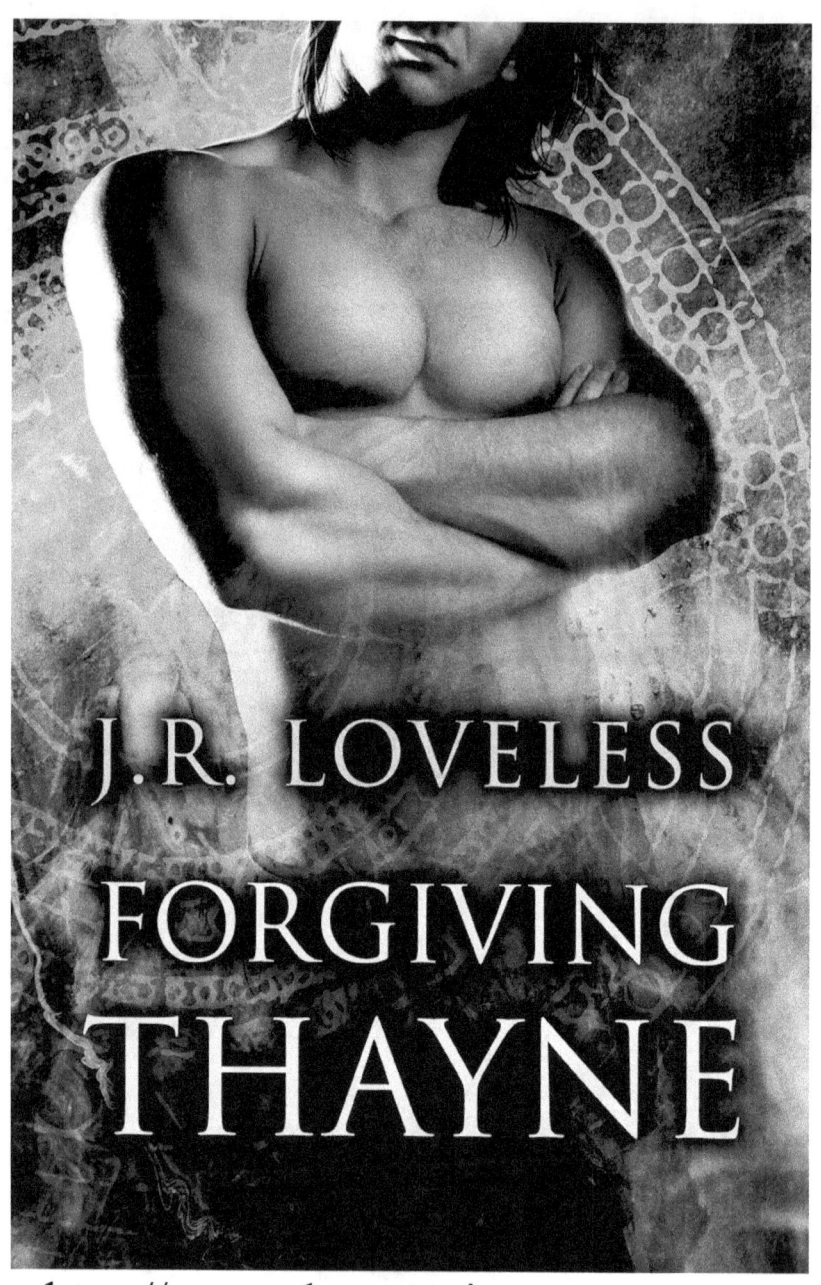

J.R. LOVELESS

FORGIVING
THAYNE

http://www.dreamspinnerpress.com

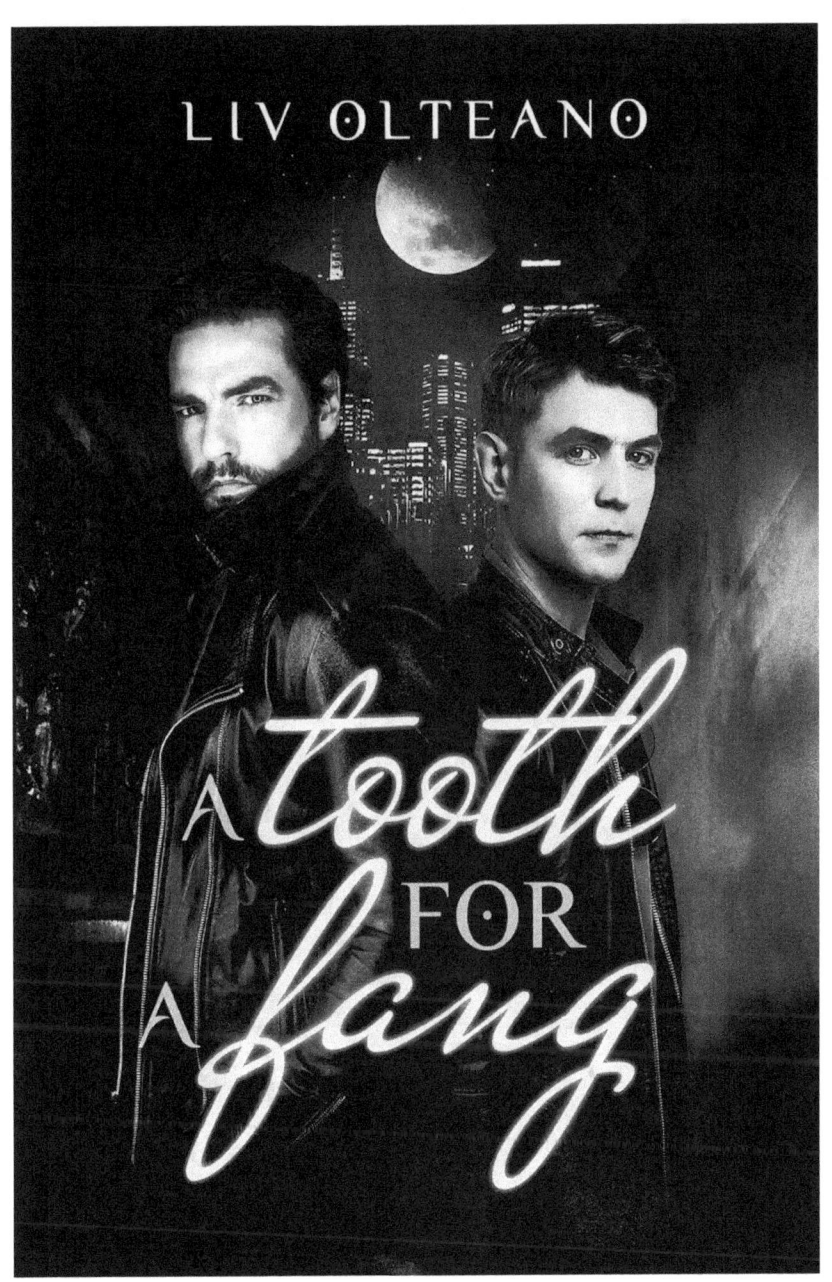

LIV OLTEANO

A tooth FOR A fang

http://www.dreamspinnerpress.com

http://www.dreamspinnerpress.com

JACQUES N. HOFF

Jay Walking

http://www.dreamspinnerpress.com

THE
GENERAL AND THE
ELEPHANT CLOCK
OF AL-JAZARI

SARAH BLACK

http://www.dreamspinnerpress.com

NO
COMMITMENT
Necessary

TALIA CARMICHAEL

ENCOUNTERS

THE WAY
THINGS ARE

A.J. THOMAS

http://www.dreamspinnerpress.com

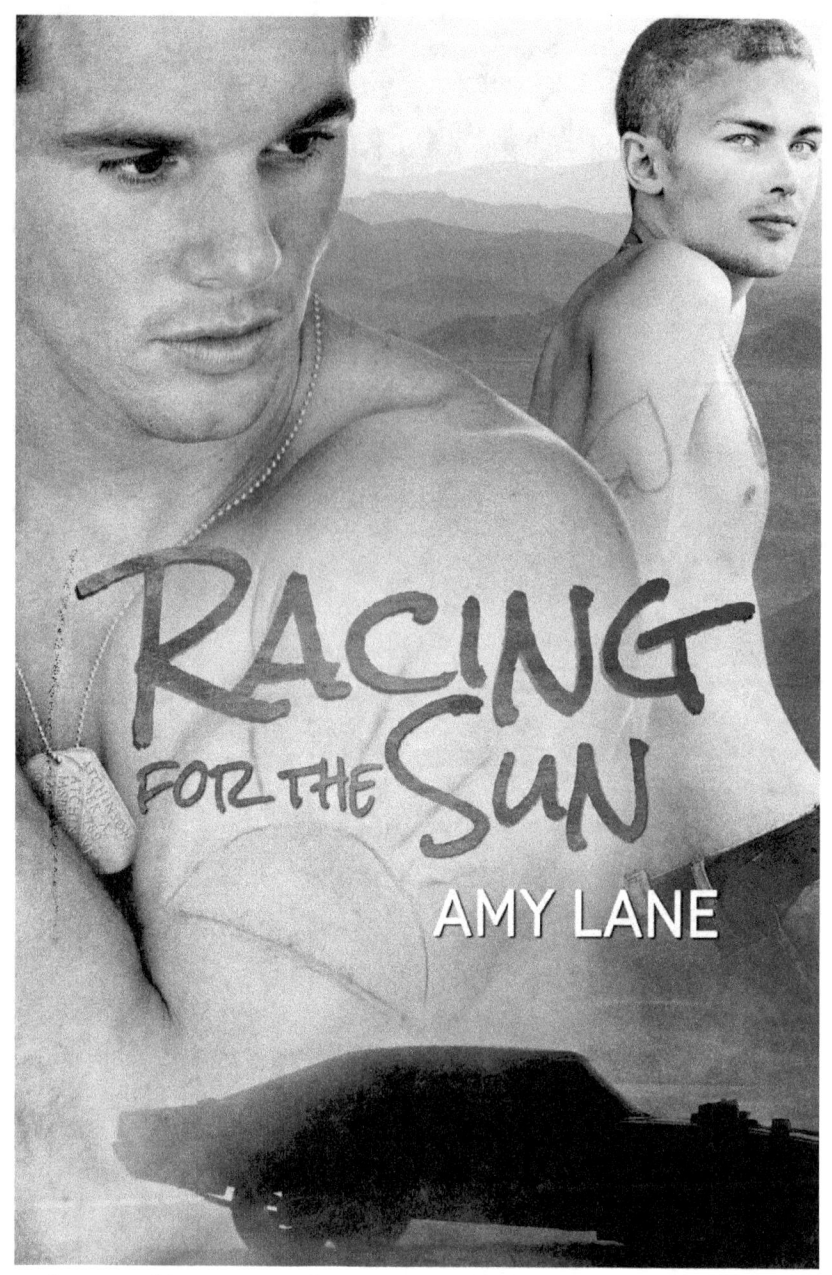

Racing
for the Sun

AMY LANE

Chasing
SUNRISE
THE DARKMORE SAGA 1
LEX CHASE

http://www.dreamspinnerpress.com

www.ingramcontent.com/pod-product-compliance
Lightning Source LLC
Chambersburg PA
CBHW060101260626
47160CB00005B/1744